THE MYSTERY OFF GLEN ROAD

Trixie
Belden

Your TRIXIE BELDEN Library

1 The Secret of the Mansion
2 The Red Trailer Mystery
3 The Gatehouse Mystery
4 The Mysterious Visitor
5 The Mystery Off Glen Road
6 Mystery in Arizona
7 The Mysterious Code
8 The Black Jacket Mystery
9 The Happy Valley Mystery
10 The Marshland Mystery
11 The Mystery at Bob-White Cave
12 The Mystery of the Blinking Eye
13 The Mystery on Cobbett's Island
14 The Mystery of the Emeralds
15 Mystery on the Mississippi
16 The Mystery of the Missing Heiress
17 The Mystery of the Uninvited Guest
18 The Mystery of the Phantom Grasshopper
19 The Secret of the Unseen Treasure
20 The Mystery Off Old Telegraph Road
21 The Mystery of the Castaway Children
22 Mystery at Mead's Mountain
23 The Mystery of the Queen's Necklace
24 Mystery at Saratoga
25 The Sasquatch Mystery
26 The Mystery of the Headless Horseman
27 The Mystery of the Ghostly Galleon
28 The Hudson River Mystery
29 The Mystery of the Velvet Gown
30 The Mystery of the Midnight Marauder
31 Mystery at Maypenny's
32 The Mystery of the Whispering Witch *(new)*
33 The Mystery of the Vanishing Victim *(new)*
34 The Mystery of the Missing Millionaire *(new)*

Trixie Belden and the MYSTERY OFF GLEN ROAD

BY JULIE CAMPBELL

Cover by Jack Wacker

GOLDEN PRESS
Western Publishing Company, Inc.
Racine, Wisconsin

ISBN 0-307-21534-2

CONTENTS

THE MYSTERY OFF GLEN ROAD

Blowing for Trouble • 1

IT'S SUPER-GLAMOROUS perfect, Honey," Trixie said with satisfaction. "I never thought we'd get it all done before Thanksgiving, did you?"

"It seemed to take forever," Honey Wheeler agreed.

The two girls were surveying the interior of their newly finished clubhouse. They belonged to a teen-age group and called themselves the B.W.G.'s—short for the Bob-Whites of the Glen. Other members were Trixie's brothers, Brian and Mart; Honey's adopted brother, Jim Frayne; and pretty Di Lynch.

In the days of carriages and sleighs, the small cottage had been the gatehouse of the huge estate that now belonged to the Wheelers. The Manor House, as it was called, formed the western boundary of Crabapple Farm, the Beldens' property. Both homes faced Glen Road and were about two miles from the village of Sleepyside, a small Westchester town that nestled among the rolling hills on the east bank of the Hudson River.

All of the B.W.G.'s attended the junior-senior high school in town, where Mr. Belden worked in the bank. Trixie and Honey were both thirteen, but they didn't look at all alike. Trixie was small and sturdily built, with round blue eyes and short sandy curls. Her best friend was tall and slim with enormous hazel eyes. She had shoulder-length golden brown hair, which had earned for her the nickname Honey. She loved to sew, and it was she who had made the attractive curtains that Trixie had just helped her hang at the windows.

The boys had recently put a new roof on the clubhouse, painted it both inside and out, and partitioned off one section of the interior, which they had lined with shelves. Here the boys and girls kept their winter and summer sports equipment: skis, skates, hockey sticks, sleds, pup tents, tennis rackets, and the like. Brian and Jim, who were older and good at carpentry, had made a big table and benches for the conference room, using odds and ends of pine that they bought very cheaply at the Sleepyside lumberyard. Mart, who was eleven months older than Trixie, was not as handy with carpentry tools as the other boys were, but he had done his share by sanding and staining the furniture.

The cottage had a dirt floor, which they hoped to cover someday with wide boards, but right now there remained not a cent in the treasury. A rule of the club was that no member could contribute money that she or he had not earned. Although Honey's father was very rich, she had earned her share of what was needed for the necessary repairs through mending jobs. Jim, who had inherited half a million dollars from a great-uncle, had worked as hard as the Belden boys, serving as a handyman after school and on weekends. Earning the money themselves had meant, of course, that there was very little time left for work on the clubhouse, but at last it was finished.

Trixie had put into the treasury every week the five dollars that her father gave her for doing household chores and helping her mother take care of mischievous six-year-old Bobby Belden. Because she hated any kind of indoor work and was very apt to lose patience if Bobby were left in her care for too long, Trixie sometimes felt that she had worked harder than anyone else. But it had been worth all of their efforts because the clubhouse was now a "dream cottage."

"Only one thing is lacking," Trixie said to Honey. "Heat. Now that Indian summer is over, it's going to be so cold in the evenings that we'll have to wear fur coats when we hold meetings."

Honey giggled. "Not that any of us has a fur coat! But the boys are wonderful trappers. Maybe they'll catch a couple of million mink for us. The streams on our property are filled with mink. Daddy hates them because they eat up all his trout." She backed out of the cottage and stared at it speculatively. "The evergreens protect it from the wind, but you're right, Trixie. It will soon be too cold for us to sit around. Up until now, we've all been working so hard we haven't noticed how chilly it gets after sundown." She shivered and slipped her arms into the sleeves of the sweater she had been wearing over her slim shoulders. "B-r-r. This wind is an icy blast."

Trixie nodded. "It was a gentle zephyr when we went inside early this morning." She closed the clubhouse door and slipped on her own sweater. "Wow! It's eleven o'clock, Honey. If this wind keeps up, it means we're in for a hurricane."

Honey sighed. "And only yesterday it was so hot we were wearing shorts and blouses." They linked arms and started up the sloping lawn to the big house. "Speaking of clothes, we'd better start getting ready for the wedding reception. The ceremony is at noon."

"I know," Trixie said mournfully. "I wish we could go just as we are. I never feel comfortable in anything but jeans. But I suppose I'll have to wear a dress today."

Celia, the Wheelers' pretty little maid, was getting married that day to Tom Delanoy, the handsome young chauffeur. After a wedding breakfast at the Manor House, they were going off on a two-week honeymoon. On their return, they would make their home in the *Robin*, a luxurious red trailer that was parked on the hill above the stable. The *Robin* had once belonged to Mr. Lynch, whose daughter, Diana, had recently been admitted to the club.

"I wish I had enough money to buy Celia and Tom a wedding present," Trixie said to Honey. "Moms and Dad are giving them those Adirondack blankets they wanted, but I'd like to give them something on my own." She reached into the pocket of her jeans and produced a grimy dime. "Do you think a box of toothpicks would be appreciated?"

Honey hugged her arm. "You're so funny, Trix. Every time you hand over your money to the club, you make a big fuss, but deep down underneath, you're the most generous girl in the world."

Trixie flushed with pleasure. "I'm not generous at all," she mumbled. "I'm terribly selfish. I don't help Moms half as much as I should. If we were rich like you, it would be different, but Moms does everything, and she never complains. Even when she's canning gallons of stuff all day in boiling hot weather, she always looks so young and pretty. When I do help, I moan and groan. Honestly, Honey, half the time when Dad gives me that five dollars, I feel so guilty I wouldn't take it if it weren't for the club."

"Well, I think you work very hard and deserve it," Honey said loyally. "But you'd better hurry home now." She started up the steps to the wide veranda, and Trixie raced off down the path to her little white farmhouse in the hollow.

There she found that Brian and Mart had just finished putting up the storm windows. They were carrying a long ladder down the terrace steps and greeted her with sour expressions on their faces.

Mart, although several inches taller than Trixie, looked enough like her to have been her twin. He wore his sandy hair in a short cut; if he hadn't, it would have been as curly as Trixie's and Bobby's. He narrowed his blue eyes and said out of the corner of his mouth, "Where have you been, if I may be so bold as to ask? You were supposed to wash the storm windows before we put them up."

"Oh, is that so?" Trixie demanded, although she knew perfectly well that it was so; she had simply forgotten.

"Yes, it is so!" Brian tiredly pushed a lock of his

wavy jet black hair out of his eye.

"Say," Mart yelled, "hang on to your end with both hands, please. This wind will snatch the ladder away from us if you don't watch out."

Brian grabbed the swaying ladder, and the wind promptly blew the lock of hair back into his eye. He glared at Trixie. "We don't mind doing men's work, which in this gale was *super*men's work, but when we have to do women's work, too—ugh. I think the domestic help should be more reliable."

Trixie sniffed. "Help is right. That's just what I am. I slave from morning to night, making beds, dusting and washing dishes, while you two—"

"Dusting dishes?" Mart elevated his sandy eyebrows. "Come, come, young woman. No dish in our house stays on a shelf long enough to collect dust." He licked his lips hungrily. "Personally, I can't wait for that wedding breakfast. Which *you* are going to miss."

"Wha-at?" Trixie, buffeted by the gale, had been trailing them up the driveway toward the garage. Now she stopped dead in her tracks, and the wind almost blew her flat. "Oh, no, Mart!" she gasped. "I *am* going to the breakfast. Don't tell me I'm going to be punished because I forgot to wash the storm windows. Moms and Dad wouldn't be so cruel."

He glanced at her over one shoulder. "Our parents have not yet been informed of how remiss you were." Mart, who considered himself far superior to Trixie mentally, loved to use big words when he talked to her. "Brian and I are not what, in the vernacular, would be termed tattletales. So we have decided to mete out justifiable punishment in our own way. Namely, we have priority on the shower. Under normal circumstances, since we are gentlemen of the first water, we would bow to the ancient and honorable rule concerning precedent in such matters—that is, ladies first. But since you are certainly not a lady, you will be constrained to refrain from ablutions, which are all too obviously indicated, until we have abluted and disported ourselves in the shower. Thus, to put it simply for the simpleminded, you haven't a prayer of getting ready in time for the wedding breakfast."

Trixie stuck out her tongue at him. "Oh, go jump in the lake."

"That," Mart said emphatically, "is just what *you* should do. Complete with a cake of soap and a scrubbing brush."

"Correct," Brian agreed. "True, the water in the Wheelers' lake will be very cold on a day like this, but it's your only chance, Trix. Moms and Bobby have established priority on the bathtub for the next hour. Dad is now occupying the shower room. When he departs, I and Mart, in that order, take over." He set the ladder against a wall in the garage. "By the time you are bathed and dressed, there will be nothing left of the breakfast except a turkey carcass and a ham bone."

"I don't agree," Mart interrupted as they went out into the wind again. "The ham bone goes to Jim's springer spaniel, Patch. All parts of the turkey carcass that are not injurious to canines go to our own Irish setter, Reddy." He shrugged. "Trixie can, of course, nibble on bones that are apt to splinter in the stomach and cause canine digestive disturbances. For example, the drumsticks, but since those are our favorite portions, Brian, I doubt—"

"Oh, stop it!" Trixie exploded. "I don't care if I am late at the breakfast; there'll still be tons to eat. The Wheelers are giving it, remember?" She ran up the terrace steps and into the kitchen. The wind snatched the door out of her hands, banged it against the wall of the house, and then slammed it shut.

Oh, dear, Trixie thought as she climbed the stairs, *I'll get the blame for that. I get the blame for everything.* In the upstairs hall she stopped, her self-pity overwhelmed by a sense of guilt. She had not only promised to wash the storm windows that morning, but she had assured her mother that she would bathe Bobby and dress him in his Sunday suit.

Judging from the sounds that were coming out

of the bathroom, there could be no doubt that Bobby was now being scrubbed from head to toe under violent protest. His shrieks rose above the roar of the wind.

"Holp, holp!" Bobby was yelling. "Mummy, you've rub-ded off my ear, and I got soap in my eyes. Holp! I'm drownding. I'm drownding! Holp! Holp!"

From the adjoining shower room came very different sounds. Mr. Belden was singing a happy song at the top of his lungs. "He's singing," Trixie muttered miserably, "so he can't hear Bobby's shrieks. He's going to be furious with me because Moms will be a wreck when she's finished with Bobby. What made me stay at the clubhouse so long? Honey didn't really need me. Brian and Mart are right. I don't deserve to go to the wedding breakfast. I'll stay home, instead, and vacuum the whole house and scrub and wax the kitchen linoleum. I'll even—"

Then suddenly, above Bobby's yells and Mr. Belden's gay song, came another sound that drowned out all others. It was a deafening crash.

Trixie fled to the nearest window. What she saw made her close her eyes and sink to the floor on her knees. One of the ancient crab apple trees that lined the driveway had been uprooted by the gale. If it had fallen a few seconds sooner, Brian and Mart would have been buried under the debris!

The Wedding Breakfast • 2

TRIXIE RACED DOWN to the driveway and found that Brian and Mart were staring in awed amazement at the uprooted crab apple tree. It had fallen so close to them that the outer branches had scratched their faces.

"Wow!" Mart finally got out. "That *was* kind of close."

Trixie, in order to hide her own horror at the near-catastrophe, said tartly, "Well, at least you won't have to shave now, Brian. There's not a speck of fuzz on your face, which, I might add, is as pale as a ghost's, in spite of your tan."

"You look pretty ghostly yourself," he retorted.

"Ghastly is the word," Mart said.

"Yes, yes," Trixie said airily. "I feel I'm going to faint. I'd best take a shower right away. It's the only thing that'll revive me."

"Okay, you win," they said in unison. "We have to get rid of this mess before we do anything."

"However," Mart added, shaking a stern finger at Trixie, "let it be strictly understood, my dear sibling, that you are *not* to eat everything before we manage to drag our weary bodies up to the Manor House."

"I'll do my best," Trixie replied. "Let's see now, what did you say? The ham bone for Patch and the turkey carcass for Reddy. When I've finished with the drumsticks, I'll wrap them in waxed paper and treasure them for you." She scampered off, chuckling to herself.

But, as it turned out, all of the Beldens were among the early arrivals at the reception. Guests came not only from the immediate neighborhood and from Sleepyside, but also from towns up the river. Some of those in the latter group, friends and relatives of the bride and groom, were delayed by the Sunday traffic and arrived long after Brian and Mart appeared.

Celia, looking prettier than ever in her white gown of lace over satin, and Tom, looking like a movie star in his rented cutaway, greeted the guests. Trixie was surprised to find Mr. and Mrs.

Wheeler were not in the receiving line, as had originally been planned.

"Daddy was called away on business at the last minute," Honey said in answer to Trixie's question. "To Florida, and so Mother just couldn't resist going along. All planes have been grounded on account of this terrible wind, so they're driving as far as Washington and taking a plane from there."

"I keep telling you it's a hurricane," Trixie said. "We've already lost a crab apple, and Dad says we'll probably lose more before the wind dies down. Some of them are more than a hundred years old. Moms is in tears about it. They're so beautiful in the spring when the blossoms 'snow' all over the place." She stopped suddenly and grabbed Honey's arm. "Oh, woe! Some of those evergreens down by the clubhouse are ancient, too. Suppose one of them crashes into the cottage!"

Honey covered her face with her slim hands. "Let's not even think about such a horrible thing. The walls aren't really much stronger than those toothpicks you were going to give Celia and Tom as a wedding present."

"But there must be something we can do," Trixie cried. "Now that the boys have eaten just about everything in sight, I suggest we have an emergency conference."

"You all go ahead," Honey said. "I can't leave

Miss Trask to cope with everything by herself. She has to take not only Mother's place as hostess, but also Celia's place as the downstairs maid! You know what a good sport she is, Trixie. I've got to help her now."

Miss Trask, who had originally been Honey's governess, ran the whole huge estate, together with Regan, the redheaded groom. Honey's mother, who looked exactly as Honey would in another twenty years, was not very strong, and, as she often said herself, she couldn't boil water without burning it. Mr. Wheeler was called away so frequently on business trips that he was only too glad to leave the management of the Manor House in the capable hands of Miss Trask and Regan.

"I don't know what your parents would do without Miss Trask and Regan," Trixie said to Honey. "But what about that cross-looking gamekeeper your father just hired? It doesn't seem like him to hire someone without Regan's approval. What cooks, anyway, Honey?"

Honey sighed. "It's all so involved. Ever since summer, Daddy has been buying up land on both sides of Glen Road, so now he has a sanctuary of about three hundred acres. You know how he loves to hunt and shoot and fish. Well, it's stocked with all sorts of creatures like deer and pheasant and partridge and trout and bass, which cost a small fortune—more even than the land itself, I guess. So, when one of Daddy's friends recommended Mr. Fleagle as the best gamekeeper in the world, Daddy snapped him up."

"Oh, well, I suppose he's all right," Trixie said cheerfully. "But you can see that Regan doesn't like him. They've been glowering at each other ever since Fleagle arrived."

"Regan," Honey confided in a whisper, "*despises* him. And since they have to share the apartment above the garage, the situation is impossible. They squabble from morning till night, mainly because Fleagle thinks he can take a horse from the stable whenever he feels like it."

Trixie shuddered elaborately. Regan was a great friend of all the B.W.G.'s and had helped them out of many scrapes. But, like Jim and Mr. Wheeler, he had a temper quick to flare up—although just as quick to subside—and so they were very careful never to disobey his orders. "I wouldn't dare take even an inch of old leather out of the stable without having Regan's permission," Trixie said, "and neither would you, Honey Wheeler."

Honey nodded. "Fleagle thinks he's just wonderful. Not Regan, Fleagle, if you know what I mean. He claims that he can't patrol the game preserve any way except on horseback, which is true, because there aren't any roads wide enough for a jeep—just winding paths and trails." She glanced worriedly through the French doors at the two big, broad-shouldered men who were out on the veranda now, obviously in the midst of a heated argument. "If only Fleagle would be more polite. *You* know, consult Regan before he goes riding off on Jupiter or Strawberry. The worst part of it," she finished exasperatedly, "is that when Fleagle comes back with a horse all sweaty, he refuses to groom him or clean the tack."

It was Trixie's turn to cover her face with her hands. "I'm surprised Fleagle is alive," she gasped. "Regan would draw and quarter us if we returned a horse to the stable and didn't groom said horse and saddle-soap every inch of leather."

"I know," Honey said with a wan smile. "But Fleagle thinks he's above such menial chores. Trying to keep those two men from each other's throats is driving Miss Trask out of her mind. Look!"

Miss Trask was the brisk kind of woman who, no matter what the occasion was, always wore tailored suits and sensible oxfords. She seldom wore a hat over her short gray hair and liked nothing better than to take long walks in the pouring rain, spurning an umbrella as something beneath her dignity. Usually her bright blue eyes had a merry twinkle in them, but they were somberly dark as she joined the two angry men on the veranda. Trixie could see that Miss Trask's face was lined with worry as she struggled against the wind to close the French doors behind her.

"Gleeps," Trixie said to Honey, "she *does* need your help. With Tom off on his wedding trip, Miss Trask will have to do all of the chauffeuring, too."

"That's right," Honey agreed. "It's no secret how much Regan hates cars. Besides, what with Fleagle causing him so much extra work, Regan couldn't possibly do any driving. I'm really glad Mother and Daddy have gone off in the limousine. At least nobody has to drive Daddy to the station and back every day." She pulled Trixie out into the hall. "The thing that scares me to death is this: Suppose Regan quits. He's fed up to the teeth with Fleagle. Miss Trask and I hoped to tell Daddy today that he's got to fire that gamekeeper, but Mother and Daddy left before we had a chance."

Trixie shuddered again. "If Regan quits, our lives are ruined. Your father would sell the horses in no time flat, because, of course, there just isn't any groom in the whole wide world like Regan."

"More than that," Honey continued, "there are very few people who are as understanding as Regan is. I mean, we're really awful nuisances, in spite of the fact that we try not to be. Some weeks we exercise the horses every single day, rain or shine. Then all of a sudden, not one of us goes near the stable.

Like during exams, or when the boys spent every spare minute shingling the clubhouse roof. Or when they were painting the walls and building the shelves and making the furniture. You and I did ride then, after school and sometimes before breakfast, but we didn't exercise Jupe and Starlight. So Regan had to, and although he didn't complain, I know he was furious. The thing is, he wouldn't mind so much if we didn't wait until the last minute to let him know whether we're going to ride or not."

Trixie sank down on the bottom step of the staircase. "I don't know how Regan stands us," she admitted. "We Bob-Whites have got to pull ourselves together and make more sense. We'd better have a conference right away."

Honey giggled nervously. "You just said that, only you were talking about the hurricane. Here come the boys now. You bring them up to date on everything, Trixie. I've got to go back to the dining room and make sure that the coffee is hot and the punch cold." With a gay wave, she edged past Jim and was lost in the crowded living room.

Jim, flanked by Brian and Mart, marched down the hall and came to a stop beside Trixie. "You girls are up to something," Jim said, pretending to be very stern. "I can tell. What *have* you done?"

Trixie scrambled to her feet, tripped, and sprawled headlong. Nobody said anything for a long minute as she lay there, overwhelmed by rage, frustration, and embarrassment.

Mart turned to Brian. "Since we are unfortunately related to that object, is it not up to us to restore her to some semblance of equilibrium before the wedding guests trample her to a pulp?"

"Well, I don't know," Brian said soberly. "She might be more useful as a pulp. When cleaning storm windows, for instance, a spongelike substance comes in mighty handy."

"True," Mart agreed and nudged Trixie's ankle with his toe. "But until she is mashed into the proper shape, might she not prove to be a dangerous hazard to myopic guests, who could mistake her for a one-dimensional article of furniture, perhaps part of the carpet?"

"I doubt that," Brian replied. "In that strangely feminine garment she is wearing, she looks more like a giant but bruised California orange. In my opinion—"

"Oh, stop it, you two!" Jim exploded with laughter. He reached down two strong arms and helped Trixie to her feet. As he settled her back on the step, he said, "Do you feel as though you broke any bones when you salaamed to us so gracefully?"

Trixie glared at him. "I didn't salaam or break any bones, smarty. It's this party dress Moms made me wear. I'm going to take it right off so Brian and

Mart can use it for cleaning windows."

"Oh, *no*," Mart yelped. "Not here and now. In the words of the Ancient Mariner: 'O wedding guest, O wedding guest, tarry awhile, said Slow.' "

Trixie turned to glare at him. "You've got it all mixed up with an old nursery rhyme. I think it's 'Polly Put the Kettle on and We'll All Have Tea.' "

"Let's do have tea," Jim said easily. "Punch, anyway. It's got a tea base. Would you like me to bring you a glass, Trix?"

"No," Trixie shouted impatiently. "I couldn't eat or drink another thing." She leaned forward slightly. "Listen, you dopes. There's an awful storm raging outside, just in case you haven't noticed. That blue spruce, which is almost a part of our clubhouse, must be even older than the Ancient Mariner. The wind is blowing from the east. Suppose it—"

"Gleeps," Mart interrupted, suddenly very serious. "She's right, men. Is there anything we can do?"

Brian sank down on the step beside Trixie. "We could wire it to another evergreen, but they're all Ancient Mariners, aren't they, Jim?"

Jim nodded. "If we wired the spruce to one of the pines, we'd simply have twin hazards."

"Tweedledum and Tweedledee," Mart said sadly. "As in *Alice in Wonderland*."

"I wish you'd learn to quote correctly," Trixie snapped. "The proper quotation at the moment is what happened to Humpty Dumpty. If any one of those evergreens falls on our clubhouse, all of the king's horses and all of the king's men will never be able to put it together again."

"Not without a king's ransom," Jim agreed. "And since none of us has a penny at the moment—"

Trixie couldn't help laughing. Jim was just wonderful. There he was, rich enough in his own right to buy and sell dozens of clubhouses, but he always acted as though he were just as poor as the Beldens. It all came from the fact that, before the Wheelers adopted him, he had been a homeless, half-starved orphan. The money that he had inherited about the same time, he had put away into a trust fund so that when he was graduated from college, he could launch his favorite project: an outdoor school for underprivileged orphan boys. Brian, whose ambition was to become a doctor, had already agreed to be the school physician. Mart, after he was graduated from an upstate agricultural college, was going to be in charge of the farming end of the project.

Thinking about Mart's career made Trixie whirl on him. "You're supposed to know something about trees," she cried. "Can't you pull your addled brains together and think up some sort of solution to our problem?"

He bowed stiffly. "Like George Washington, I cannot tell a lie. There is no—"

"Hatchets," Trixie interrupted in a loud voice. "Let's all dash down to the clubhouse and chop down all the trees." She started to get up, but Jim gently pushed her back. She looked up, puzzled.

"Pull *your* addled brains together, Trix," he cautioned her. "The trees, as well as the clubhouse, belong to Dad. Remember? Since he's not here to give us permission, we can't behave like vandals. It's just possible that he more highly values those beautiful old evergreens than he does a ramshackle cottage that he never saw until you and Honey discovered it."

It all seemed so hopeless that Trixie could hardly keep from crying. She could tell from the stubborn look on Jim's face that there was no point in arguing. He was just one of those people who were so honorable that they leaned over backward to respect other people's rights, even when it made no sense.

The wind was truly roaring now, rattling the windows and howling down the chimneys of the old house. Trixie was positive that in the morning not one of Mr. Wheeler's prized old evergreens would be left standing. And beneath the debris would be the remnants of their clubhouse.

Trixie stood up, being very careful not to trip again. "Toothpicks," she said succinctly.

Mart closed his hand around her brown wrist.

"One of the nicest *non sequiturs* I've ever heard. Elucidate, my dear sister. Pray do."

Trixie jerked away from him. "Praying," she said, "is just what you boys should do. Otherwise, when you go down to the clubhouse tomorrow morning before school, you're going to find nothing to show for all our work except a ten-cent box of toothpicks!"

Break of a Lifetime • 3

ALL AFTERNOON the wind blew with wild fury. Because the Belden property was down in a hollow, only very old trees were uprooted. But in the woods on the high land behind the Manor House, many valuable trees, unprotected from the fierce wind, were damaged and killed.

At five-thirty, the sixty-mile-an-hour-plus gale dropped to forty and finally slowed to ten miles an hour. Not until then were the Bob-Whites permitted to leave the house and survey the damage. The bridle path that led up from the stable to the red trailer was blocked by the trunks and branches of trees. Regan and the gamekeeper, Fleagle, were clearing away the debris, and they were arguing as usual.

When the boys offered to help, Fleagle glared at them. "Scram, you kids," he growled. "You'll just be in the way. This path must be cleared before tomorrow morning so I can ride into the game preserve and find out what damage has been done there. *That's* the most important thing."

Regan, his big freckled hands on his hips, lost his redheaded temper. "Sez you! This is only a lull in the storm. Things are going to get a lot worse tonight. Chances are good that the electric and phone wires will be down. The important thing is to do whatever we can to keep *that* from happening."

"Is there anything we *can* do?" Jim asked. "It seems pretty hopeless to me."

"It is pretty hopeless," Regan agreed. "When electric wires are torn down by falling trees, there's always the danger of fire, too. It makes me sick to think about the honeymooners' trailer. Everything those kids own—their nice wedding presents and all—could be nothing but a heap of ashes if a crackling live wire gets to lashing around in the woods."

Trixie shuddered at the mental picture. "We can't let that happen to Celia and Tom," she moaned.

"That we can't," Regan said emphatically. "So Fleagle, here, and I are going to clear a path to the trailer and tote back to the big house everything we can. Aren't we, Fleagle?" he finished in a menacing tone of voice.

For answer, the surly gamekeeper shouldered his ax and stalked back toward the garage. Over one shoulder he said, "Play Santa Claus if you like. I'm quitting."

"Oh, no," Honey moaned. "Do you think he means it, Regan?"

The groom shrugged his broad shoulders. "Whether he quits or not won't make much difference for the next few days. Unless this lull lasts, which it won't, nobody will be able to get into the game preserve on either side of the road to do any patrolling until the paths have been cleared."

Jim nodded soberly. "The power and phone companies will send out crews to repair damage to their cables, and the state will send crews to clear the main roads. But private property owners will have to cope individually after that."

"Right," said Regan, "and to hire private crews is going to run into big money. But let's not cross any bridges until we come to them. Since His Royal Highness Fleagle has quit, you boys help me clear the path to the red trailer."

"We'd like to help, too," Honey said. "Trixie and I—"

"No," Regan interrupted firmly. "This weird light

in the sky is going to fade any minute, and then it'll be pitch-dark. The velocity of the wind may suddenly increase to what it was before, with gusts of one hundred miles an hour. You girls had better go home."

Reluctantly, Trixie and Honey left. "Let's go down and see if everything's all right at the clubhouse," Trixie said, as soon as they were out of earshot. At that very moment, a sudden gust of wind flattened a white birch ahead of them and seemed to blow the gray green light out of the sky. It was, as Regan had predicted, pitch-dark, and, to make matters worse, the lights inside the Manor House went out, indicating a power failure.

Honey moved closer to Trixie. "I can't see a thing," she whispered, "and it feels as though we're going to have thunder and lightning. Let's go inside."

Trixie giggled. "Let's. But which way is inside? I feel as though we were in a giant's pocket." And then she saw a light in the kitchen, and at the same time one in the apartment over the garage. Both Miss Trask and Fleagle, Trixie could see through the windows, had lighted kerosene lamps. Miss Trask joined them on the path in a few minutes.

She handed Trixie a flashlight and said, "You'd better run along home, dear. Your mother will be worried. The phones are out of order, too."

"Thanks," Trixie said, accepting the flashlight. She hurried down the stony path to the hollow. She entered the house through the door to the kitchen, where a small kerosene lamp had been lighted. Her mother was trimming the wick of another, and her father was in the cellar, filling a kerosene heater. Logs were crackling merrily in the living-room fireplace, and Bobby was kneeling on the hearth.

"It's so 'citing," he greeted Trixie. "We're right smack in the middle of a horrorcane."

"*Horror*cane is right," Trixie said, thinking about the clubhouse. But, thank goodness, it was down on the same level with her own home, so perhaps the trees around it would still be standing in the morning.

"Where are the boys?" Mr. Belden asked as he emerged from the cellar. Trixie explained that they were helping Regan, and he said, "Well, all right, but charity begins at home. The temperature is dropping rapidly, and with the electricity off, we are helpless so far as heat, water, cooking, refrigeration, and lights are concerned."

"I can't bear to think about the meat and vegetables in the freezer," Mrs. Belden said.

"They'll be all right for a couple of days," Mr. Belden told her, "but what worries me is that the water pipes may freeze. We must, at all costs, keep the house warm, and that means fires in all of the fireplaces, because we haven't a great deal of kerosene on hand."

Trixie chuckled. "Well, one thing we do have plenty of is wood. Water, too. Brian and Mart can tote all we'll need from the brook and the cistern."

"It'll have to be strained and boiled before we can drink it," Mrs. Belden pointed out. "That means using up kerosene, and, with everyone in the whole county in the same fix, we may not be able to buy any kerosene tomorrow when the stores open."

"We can get some the very first thing from Mr. Lytell," Trixie said. "He'll probably give us neighbors priority."

"That's true," her father agreed. "And he's open on Sundays. I think I'll drive to his store now and buy several gallons." He started for the kitchen door. "When the boys get back," he said to his wife, "send them right out for wood and water. Trixie can help by carrying a light for them. I'll try to buy some flashlight batteries from Mr. Lytell, too."

After he had gone, Bobby announced, "I'll holp. I can carry my very own flashlight, 'cept that there's only one battery in it. Why do flashlights *have* to have two batteries, Trix?"

"I don't know, Bobby," Trixie said impatiently. "Ask Brian or Mart. The whole business about electricity is over my head. I don't even understand what makes an automobile run."

"I don't, either," Mrs. Belden said with a rueful smile.

"Oh, Moms," Trixie cried, "you're forever making our cars run by doing something to the spark plugs with a bobby pin."

"I don't really know what I'm doing, though," Mrs. Belden said. "But Brian does. What he doesn't know about cars isn't worth knowing. I'm so glad he has at last earned the money to buy that old car Mr. Lytell wants to sell. If ever a boy deserves to own a car of his own, that boy is Brian Belden."

Trixie nodded. "And Tom Delanoy says it's a wonderful buy at fifty dollars. Mr. Lytell's jalopy, I mean. If Mr. Lytell sold it to a secondhand dealer, that's all he'd get, but if Brian wanted to buy it from the dealer, it would cost eighty or a hundred dollars. It's one of the breaks of a lifetime, Tom says."

"And Tom knows what he's talking about," Mrs. Belden agreed. "He knows as much about cars as Regan does about horses." She stared out of the kitchen window. "I'm worried about the honeymooners, Trixie. They were driving to Canada, you know. The last thing we heard over the radio before the power failed was that falling trees were making most highways so dangerous that motorists were warned to stay off them." She lowered her voice. "I'm worried about your father and the boys, too, Trixie. I wish they were safe at home."

"Home, down in this hollow," Trixie said, "is the safest place to be. Now that all of the ancient crab apples are gone, I don't think we'll lose any more trees, do you, Moms?"

"I don't know, Trixie," her mother replied. "The wind has been rising steadily during the last half hour. Just listen to it! I think we missed the eye of the storm, but we're going to get the tail end of it, which can be the very worst of all. You know what I mean, Trixie. You've played the game crack-the-whip often enough to know that the last person is the one who gets jerked around the most. If we get whiplash from the storm, we're bound to lose some good, sturdy trees." She sank down on the kitchen stool and covered her pretty face with her hands. "I don't think I can bear it if we lose our lovely dogwoods and white birches."

Trixie swallowed hard. She realized suddenly that she had been very selfish to think only about what might happen to the clubhouse. The same tragedy, on a much, much larger scale, might be happening to the Manor House and to Crabapple Farm. Mrs. Belden loved the trees and shrubs almost as much as she loved her children. She had cared for a great many of them herself from the day that her husband had brought them home from the nursery. And Mr. Wheeler was probably equally worried about his game preserve. Falling trees could wreck, in a few minutes, all of the bird- and animal-feeding stations Mr. Fleagle had erected. And most of the paths were probably blocked now so that nothing could be done in the way of repair work for weeks and weeks.

At that moment, Brian and Mart came in. They had groped their way down from the Manor House with the aid of a flashlight that had very weak batteries, and they looked tired, dirty, and depressed.

Brian went right to the kitchen sink and turned on the tap with the hope of washing his grimy hands. Nothing came out except a gasping, moist bubble. "Oh," he said, chagrined, "I forgot that we're completely dependent upon electricity for light, heat, and water. You can't even cook, can you, Moms? And I'm starving."

"Me, too," Bobby chimed in.

"I," said Mart, "am not starving; I am ravenous."

Mrs. Belden laughed. "What on earth happened to all of that delicious food you consumed at the wedding breakfast? But it doesn't matter. We can cook on top of the kerosene heater and broil chops over the fire in the living room. Which reminds me. You boys must bring in some wood and water right away." She turned away from the window, and Trixie heard her say to herself, "I hate to have you boys go out in that awful wind, but it just can't be helped."

Mr. Belden came back then with a five-gallon can of kerosene and some flashlight batteries. "It *sounds* worse than it really is," he said cheerfully. When he and the older boys, with Trixie helping, had brought in a good supply of water, kindling wood, and logs, he said to Brian, "Mr. Lytell showed me your jalopy. It's a good buy, son, and I'm glad you're going to get it. Congratulations! Unless this storm delays everything, your registration plate should arrive in the mail tomorrow."

"And then," Brian said dreamily, "I can drive my car home. Gosh, I just can't believe it, Dad. *My car. My very own car!*"

"You deserve it," his father said, placing one hand on Brian's shoulder. "You started out with two dollars and slowly but surely built it up to fifty. That took courage and perseverance."

"It was more than fifty dollars," Mrs. Belden pointed out, and even in the dim light of the kitchen, Trixie could see that her mother was very proud of Brian. "You're forgetting that he had to earn the money for the registration plate and the insurance, too, Peter." She smiled up at her husband. "Do you remember the ancient car we bought for our honeymoon?"

Mr. Belden roared with laughter. "If only we'd had Brian along to tell us what was wrong with it when it kept breaking down!"

Brian's handsome face was flushed with pleasure. "Ah, gee, Dad," he mumbled, "I'm not *that* good a mechanic."

But he was, Trixie knew, and he had worked very hard to earn the money so that tomorrow he could drive his car home from Mr. Lytell's store. She began to hope then that the registration plate would arrive, and that the old saying about the men who carried the United States mail was true: *Neither rain nor snow nor gloom of night can stay these couriers from the swift completion of their appointed rounds.*

A Box of Toothpicks • 4

BOBBY WAS the only member of the Belden household who slept well that night. Every hour or so the wind swooped down into the hollow and seized the little white frame house in its teeth. At times it seemed as though the panes would be rattled right out of the windows.

Trixie dozed fitfully and every now and then was startled into wide-awakeness by the sound of crashing trees. Around midnight, the furiously lashing tail of the storm left that section of the Hudson River valley and went northward to create more havoc. The temperature rose, and a gentle, soothing rain began to patter on the roof.

Trixie slept soundly after that, and when she awoke, the sun was streaming through her bedroom window.

Trixie scrambled out of bed, thinking, *Creepers! We've all overslept! I'll bet the school bus has already gone by.*

But just then Bobby came dancing into the room, singing at the top of his lungs: "No school today. No school today!"

"How do you know?" Trixie demanded. "Did the siren blow?"

He nodded his curly blond head up and down emphatically. "It blewed while I was having dry cereal with so much 'densed milk on it, it wasn't dry anymore." He made a face. "It was awful gooky stuff, Trix, so I gived it to Reddy. Reddy just 'dored it."

Trixie laughed. Any time Bobby was given something to eat that he didn't like, the Beldens' beautiful but harum-scarum Irish setter was called in to lick the plate or bowl clean. Mrs. Belden was the only one in the household who was not aware of this scheme, and so she was often amazed when Bobby frequently complained of hunger such a short while after supposedly finishing a huge meal. On those occasions, Bobby demanded—and got—thick sandwiches made of bread, butter, peanut butter, and jam. Trixie and her older brothers liked these delicious snacks just as much as Bobby did, and they had named the sandwiches the Crabapple Farm Specials.

Right now Bobby was gripping in both of his plump hands a partially eaten "special," and a great deal of the filling was on his eyebrows, cheeks, and chin. In spite of that, Trixie gave the little boy a big hug. "You're a fiend, Bobby," she said, "but you're *so* cute. Did you really hear the no-school siren? Are you sure it wasn't a fire-alarm siren?"

Bobby crammed a large portion of the "special" into his mouth and said something unintelligible. As though in answer to Trixie's question, Mart came in then. He was wearing a heavy wool sweater, jeans, high wool socks, and rubberized hunting boots. Trixie suddenly realized that, dressed as she was in nothing but flannel pajamas, she was very cold. Her teeth began to chatter, and she popped back into bed, drawing the covers up to her chin.

"Go away," she said to Mart. "If there's no school today, I may as well sleep some more."

"Not so," he said, and yanked the blankets and comforter from her bed. "Rise and shine, slave. Or perhaps I should say witch. In my opinion, you should be burned at the stake."

Trixie shivered and donned a warm bathrobe. "I can't think of anything more pleasant," she said. "The sooner and closer I can get to a roaring fire, the happier I'll be. But why do you say I'm a witch?"

He sat on the foot of her bed and pulled Bobby onto his lap. "Because your dire predictions have come true. Or should I say maledictions?"

"Oh, stop asking me silly questions," Trixie cried impatiently. "Try to speak in words of one syllable, Mart. *What's happened?*"

Mart didn't say anything for a long minute. Trixie stared at him, and now she could see that, although he had been talking lightly, the expression on his face was one of abject misery. "Mart," she cried again, "what's happened?"

He buried his face in Bobby's plump neck and said in a muffled voice, "The clubhouse. It's not exactly a box of toothpicks, but a near thing."

"Oh, no," Trixie moaned, pulling a blanket over her knees. "The blue spruce?"

Mart nodded. "It wasn't completely uprooted, thank heavens, but it gave the roof an awful beating and tore out the whole back wall. The rain didn't help matters, either. Everything is soaked."

Trixie was too horrified to speak, but Bobby squirmed away from Mart and began to chant, "I want to see. Hey! I want to see. Is there a great big 'normous hole in the roof, Mart? As big as the hole in my panda's head?"

"Yes," Mart said sadly. "Relatively speaking, the storm scalped our clubhouse as efficiently as you scalped your panda." He turned to Trixie. "Brian's down there with Jim and Honey now. Jim says it'll cost fifty bucks to fix the roof and the wall. And not one of us, except Brian, has a dime."

"Brian hasn't got a dime, either," Trixie said staunchly. "That money he saved really belongs to Mr. Lytell. For the jalopy, you know."

"*I* know," Mart admitted, "but Brian feels different now. You know how Brian is. 'United we stand; divided we fall.' *E pluribus unum* and all that sort of stuff. Sickening, but true. 'How unselfish can you get?' we all kept asking him!"

Trixie swallowed hard. "Jim and Brian *are* sickening," she finally got out. "They are always so honorable all over the place. It gets dull." She scrambled to her feet. "Anyway, Mart, Brian has just got to buy that jalopy. No matter what he says, we Bob-Whites can't touch a penny of his money."

"I got money," Bobby chanted. "I got five pennies." He reached into the pocket of his overalls and produced three very dull pennies. After counting them carefully in a loud, surprised voice, he shouted, "Hey! I losted two whole cents. Do you s'pose there's a hole in my pocket?"

"No," Trixie said firmly. "You know perfectly well that Dad pays Honey for keeping you in pockets and shoulder straps. You lost that money because you're forever turning somersaults. Now run along, Bobby. When Moms empties the vacuum cleaner bag, she'll find your pennies."

He raced off, and Mart said to Trixie, "Get dressed and meet us at the Manor House soon as you can. We're invited to a breakfast of yesterday's leftovers on the veranda."

"Yummy-yum," Trixie said hungrily. "But what about our chores? We can't leave Moms—"

"There are no chores," Mart interrupted. "The phone's working now, and the electric company says the current will be turned on early this afternoon. Until that happens, Moms says there's no sense in doing anything in the way of chores."

"Thank goodness our mother is such a good sport," said Trixie. "I couldn't possibly dust without the vacuum, because when the wind roared down our chimney, it blew ashes an inch thick all over the floors and furniture. And it'll be much easier to wash all of the dishes at once, when we have hot water in the house again."

Mart started for the door. "Moms *is* a good sport," he said, "so I guess we can't blame Brian for being one, too. It sort of runs in the family. Present company excluded, of course." He chuckled and disappeared down the hall.

Trixie donned blue jeans, a warm sweater, wool socks, and sneakers. She hurried downstairs and out to the back terrace, where she found her parents and Bobby.

"No school today for me, either," Mr. Belden said cheerfully. "Even if the bank weren't closed on account of the power failure, I couldn't get into the village without wings. There are huge trees blocking every one of the roads."

"But," Mrs. Belden put in, "the repair crews have been working since midnight, so everything will be back to normal soon. Run along, dear," she added to Trixie, "and have fun. As soon as we have electricity, we're both going to have to work like beavers."

Trixie gratefully scampered off up the path to the Manor House. The other Bob-Whites were on the veranda, munching large turkey sandwiches. They all looked so dismal that Trixie couldn't help greeting them with "Yesterday there was a wedding; today there's a wake."

"If you're referring to the wake of the storm," Jim said sourly, "you're right." He moved closer to Honey to make room for Trixie on the glider. "Here I am, loaded with money, but I can't get hold of a cent until Dad comes back from Florida."

"Oh, for pete's sake, Jim," Brian exploded, "don't start all that again. Sure, we all know that you're rich, but you inherited that money. Why do you keep on forgetting that the rule of our club is that we can't use any money that one of us didn't *earn?*"

Jim grinned. "I'm not forgetting, Brian, old boy.

But the money you want to donate, you earned for the purpose of buying a car. *Not* for the purpose of repairing one slightly wrecked clubhouse."

"That's right," Honey said. "Brian's just got to have that car. When Daddy realizes that it was our clubhouse that kept the blue spruce from being blown to the ground and uprooted, he'll give us all the money we want for fixing it up. The clubhouse, I mean. Not the spruce." She jumped up. "I'm going to borrow the money from Miss Trask right now and stop all this silly arguing."

Gently Jim pulled her back down beside him. "You'll do nothing of the kind, little stepsister," he said.

"I'm *not* your stepsister!"

Trixie could tell that kindhearted Honey was very close to tears. Trixie herself felt like crying. They couldn't accept the money that Brian had saved for his jalopy, and yet what else could they do?

"I'm your very own full-blooded, adopted sister," Honey was storming. As usual, when she was on the verge of tears, she wasn't making much sense. "What I mean is," she told Jim, "when we formed our club, we decided that we'd all be brothers and sisters. One big family was what we said, so—"

"Exactly," Brian interrupted quietly. "So, Honey, my fifty bucks belongs to all of us. A jalopy wouldn't do all of us any good, because I'm the only one who can legally do any driving." He started for the French doors to the study where the phone was. "I'm going to call up and order the wood and shingles we'll need, right now. A lot of homes were damaged by that storm. If we don't get our little order in right away, it may be months before we get any supplies. What with snow and sleet. . . ." He shrugged, went inside, and closed the doors behind him.

"Well, that's that," Mart said. "Mr. Lytell said he'd only hold the car until next Saturday. Even if all of us could get fabulously high-paying jobs for working after school between now and then, we couldn't earn fifty smackers."

"We could rob a bank," Honey suggested tearfully. "In fact, I think I will. All by myself. I'll use Bobby's water pistol. It's been done before, according to what I've read in the newspapers."

"Oh, fine," Jim said sarcastically. "Then we'll have to raise bail in order to get you out of jail."

"This is no time for rhymes," Trixie interrupted. "I have a plan that makes sense."

Mart covered his face with both hands. "Oh, no, sis, not one of those. We'll *all* end up in jail."

"That's right," Jim agreed. "Every time Trixie even thinks, we all get involved in a mystery—"

"Which," Honey put in emphatically, "Trixie always seems to solve, along with our problems. *I* think we ought to listen to her plan. Since you won't let me borrow the money from Miss Trask or rob a bank—"

Brian came back then, and Trixie said quickly, "Borrowing from Miss Trask is what gave me the idea. Mr. Fleagle is quitting, isn't he?"

"That's right," Jim said. "He left, bag and baggage, last evening during the lull in the storm."

"Well," Trixie continued, "what's to prevent us from taking over his job? For a week, anyway, until Miss Trask and Regan can manage to hire another gamekeeper."

"Say, that is a thought," Jim said. "All it would amount to would be patrolling the preserve before and after school and full time during the weekend."

Honey nodded. "Fleagle got more than fifty dollars a week for doing not much more than that. But the trouble is, Jim, Miss Trask has already put ads in the help-wanted columns of all the papers. Some truly marvelous gamekeeper may apply for the job tomorrow."

"That's right," Jim agreed. "And furthermore, we can't ask for a week's pay in advance. Even if we should get the job, we'd have to prove that we were worth fifty bucks a week."

Brian, who had been looking very happy for a moment, slumped down on a hassock near the glider. "Right, Jim," he said. "We can't do anything about the clubhouse unless we use money we have earned. So let's stop stewing about it."

Then all of a sudden Trixie remembered something. She jumped up and ran indoors, beckoning for Honey to follow her. "I've got the answer to everything," Trixie whispered as they hurried upstairs to Honey's lovely room on the second floor.

When they were seated together on the window seat, with the door to the hall closed, Trixie said, "That diamond ring Jim gave to me! If I can just get that, it'll solve all of our problems."

The Diamond Ring • 5

HONEY STARED at Trixie, her hazel eyes wide with amazement. "Are you talking about the diamond ring Jim left behind when he ran away after the Miser's Mansion burned?"

Trixie nodded. "Remember what he wrote in the note he left with it? He said I deserved it because I found it and because I saved all that money he found in the mattress from being burned."

"I certainly do remember," Honey cried excitedly. "And I see what you mean. You really *earned* that diamond ring. So if you wanted to sell it, you could use the money for fixing up the clubhouse."

"That's right," Trixie said. "But I haven't a prayer

of getting permission from Dad to sell it. He put it in our safe-deposit vault, you know, for fear I'd lose it."

"Well, then," Honey said discouragedly, "what good is it to us?"

"Plenty," Trixie told her. "I've just got to get Dad to take it out of the bank for a while. Then I can give it to Mr. Lytell as security. You know what I mean."

"No, I don't," Honey replied. "What's nosy old Mr. Lytell got to do with our wrecked clubhouse?"

"Oh, Honey," Trixie cried impatiently. "Sometimes you jump around in your conversation so fast that nobody knows what you're talking about. At other times, like now, you have a one-track mind. Can't you see that I'm talking about Brian's car?"

Honey shook with laughter. "Speaking of people who jump around in their conversation, Trixie Belden, you're much worse than I am. But now I do understand. If you give Mr. Lytell your ring as security, he'll hold the jalopy until we can earn enough money to pay Brian back the fifty dollars he loaned us. But how?" she asked. "How are you going to get your father to take the ring out of the bank?"

"That," Trixie admitted, "I've got to figure out somehow."

Honey stared vacantly around her dainty room. "If only," she said reflectively, "everyone didn't know how you hate jewelry and anything feminine.

I mean, if you were like Di Lynch and me, your father wouldn't die of surprise if you asked him if you could wear the ring for a few days. After all, it *is* yours, and almost any girl but *you* might want to wear it to a party or something."

It was Trixie's turn to shake with laughter. "You and Di," she pointed out between chuckles, "*used* to be frail and feminine, but since you two joined the Bob-Whites, I notice you both prefer blue jeans to frilly dresses." Then she sobered. "You've got something there, Honey Wheeler. My parents and Brian and Mart *would* die of amazement if I suddenly got a yen to wear joo-wells. The thing for me to do is *not* to do it too suddenly. See what I mean?"

Honey slid off the window seat and covered her face with her slim hands. "Oh, Trixie, you're so funny. You're forever telling me I don't make sense when I talk, and you almost never make sense yourself."

Trixie giggled. "I know. We're both terrible, Honey, but I'd still rather be the way we are instead of like Mart, who's forever using such big words that nobody but a college professor could ever understand what he's talking about. Mart," she added thoughtfully, "is the one I've got to fool first. That's not going to be easy. We're practically twins, you know."

Honey uncovered her face and tugged at her

bangs, frowning. "That I *do* know. In fact, you *are* twins for one whole month of the year, because your birthdays are exactly eleven months apart. But what that has to do with getting your ring out of the bank is beyond me. Please, Trixie," she begged, "try to make sense for a change."

Trixie glared at her. "I *am* making sense. Mr. Lytell has promised Brian not to sell his jalopy to a dealer until next Saturday. Between now and then, I've got to get the diamond ring so I can give it to him as security. The only way I can possibly convince Dad that I should have it is for me to go feminine all over the place. As you pointed out, I can't do that suddenly, so, between now and Friday, I've got to do it by degrees. Mart, to repeat myself, is going to be suspicious until the very end, so I've got to fool him first. Do I make myself clear?"

"Yes," Honey said in an awed tone of voice. "It's all as simple as international intrigue, and I don't think for one minute that you're going to fool anybody, let alone Mart." She grabbed Trixie's hand and dragged her over to the full-length mirror that formed the door to rows of shelves. "Just look at yourself, Trixie Belden. Did you ever see anyone who looked less frail and feminine than you?"

Trixie chortled. "I do look pretty horrible in this ragged sweater and patched jeans. And my hair should really be as long as yours and Di's—down to my shoulders, I mean. But I can't do anything about that. There just isn't going to be enough time."

Honey elevated her eyebrows. "Oh, no? That seems to me to be the simplest problem of all. You can wear a wig. One with long, black Lord Fauntleroy curls would be just the thing. Then nobody would recognize you, so nobody in your family will die of horror when suddenly you appear in a formal evening gown with a long train."

Trixie collapsed on the floor. "Let's not overdo this, Honey," she finally got out. "All I'm going to do is *not* wear ragged sweaters and patched blue jeans for a while. Instead of changing when I come home from school, I'll hang around in my school clothes."

"You can't do that," Honey objected. "You can't ride in a skirt, not without a sidesaddle, and we haven't got one, and even if we did, you wouldn't know how to cope with it. And we have to exercise the horses or Regan will be furious. He's furious enough, anyway, because now, with Fleagle gone, and Tom on his honeymoon, and Miss Trask so busy because Celia's on her honeymoon, too, he—"

"Oh, please, Honey," Trixie interrupted. "Don't go into all those complications. I'll wear jeans when we exercise the horses after school. Then I'll do just what you do—dress up for dinner. I've got some dresses somewhere, like the one that Moms made me wear to the wedding breakfast yesterday.

They're in her closet, I think, two or three of them." She got on her hands and knees and stared at her reflection in the mirror. "Maybe some perfume and lipstick would help. Earrings, too."

"Oh, definitely," Honey said, wiggling her eyebrows. "Mother's away, so we can borrow things like that by the ton. Since you refuse to wear a train and carry a lorgnette, I feel you should go in heavily for makeup. Mascara, eye shadow, eyebrow pencil, foundation creams—oh, definitely."

"Don't be sarcastic," Trixie said crossly. "This is a very serious problem, and although we're really doing it so Brian can have his jalopy, we can never let him know anything about my diamond ring. So I just have to be convincing when I ask Dad for it."

"Oh, I know," Honey cried, stooping to give Trixie a big hug. "As I keep telling you, you're just about the most generous girl who ever lived. But take my advice, Trixie. The only way you can make it convincing is for you to fall suddenly in love. That's the way it happens in books. Tomboys suddenly become ladies overnight because some man has come into their life. And," she added emphatically, "I know just the man you should fall in love with."

"Oh, no," Trixie moaned. "Not *Jim*. He's the only one of the boys who isn't, as you would say, my full-blooded brother."

"Don't be silly," Honey cried impatiently. "My cousin, Ben Riker, is the only one. You met him when we solved the red trailer mystery, and he was up here last weekend."

Trixie shuddered. "Even if he is your full-blooded cousin, I can't stand him. He's always playing horrible practical jokes."

"I know," Honey said soothingly. "He's simply ghastly, but he doesn't have to know that you've fallen in love with him. He's going to spend the Thanksgiving holidays with us, so all you have to do is pretend that you're getting in practice so that you can, well, sort of make him like you when he arrives next week."

Trixie shuddered again. "Well, if I have to for Brian's sake, I guess I have to. You know more about these things than I ever will, Honey. You'll have to coach me. How are you supposed to act when you're in love?"

"I'm not sure," Honey admitted. "But in the books, they sort of droop around the way Celia did before Tom finally asked her to marry him. And whenever you answer the phone, you don't just doodle aimlessly with a pencil. You write your name and Ben's and cancel out all the same letters in both names, and then you go through the letters that are left and say, 'Love, hate, courtship, marriage.' But if it doesn't come out right, you leave out something so it always ends with both names saying 'love' and 'marriage.' Right up until the wedding yesterday, every piece of paper in the house was covered with Celia's and Tom's names, but toward the end, all Celia wrote all over everything was simply 'Mrs. Thomas Delanoy.' "

"Oh, woe," Trixie groaned. "This is much, much more complicated than international intrigue. Do you really, honest and truly, think that if I write 'Mrs. Benjamin Riker' all over Moms's shopping list, it's going to make Dad take my diamond ring out of the bank? Instead," she answered her own question, "it'll probably make him put me into a straitjacket and have me toted off to the looney bin."

"Oh, don't be so literal, Trixie," Honey cried exasperatedly. "You know perfectly well what I mean, but you'd better start practicing now. Just swoon around and murmur to yourself, but loud enough so everybody else can hear you, 'Oh, Ben, Ben! How can I live until the Thanksgiving holidays?' "

Trixie stood up and gritted her teeth. "Blood is thicker than water, and anything for my own full-blooded brother Brian! But, Honey, I can't swoon around in this outfit. Nobody can swoon properly unless she looks a little something like the Lily Maid of Astolat, which I definitely don't."

At that moment there was a knock on Honey's bedroom door, and Mart poked his head inside.

"I've got news for you, Trix," he said. "The electricity is on, so household chores await you at home."

Trixie suddenly decided that this was as good a time as any to start trying to convince Mart that she had gone "frail and feminine."

"Chores?" she asked, buffing her stubby, slightly soiled fingernails against the ragged cuff of her sweater. "Surely you can't mean anything that might give me dishpan hands?"

Mart stared at her, openmouthed. "Wha-at did you say?" he gasped.

Trixie, trying to ignore her reflection in the mirror so she could imagine herself in a dainty frock, shook her head sorrowfully. "It isn't that I don't want to cooperate, you must understand. It's just that Ben, well, he wouldn't like it. Ben. Ah, Ben!"

If Mart had had long hair to clutch, he would have clutched it. As it was, he simply clasped his hands above his head and demanded, "Ben who, lamebrain? If you are referring to Benjamin Franklin, I've got news for you. He died before you were born and so couldn't care less if you have dishpan hands."

Honey hurried to the rescue. "Trixie's quite right, Mart," she said firmly. "Ben wouldn't like it. I mean, after all, when a girl starts wearing diamond rings, she's just got to have pretty hands. What I mean is, it's obvious, you know. Ben Riker and Trixie. It *is* obvious, isn't it? I mean, he's my own full-blooded cousin, and then Trixie is your very own full-blooded sister, so *we* should know, shouldn't we?"

Mart let out a loud groan. "So far as I am concerned, she's a full-blooded, but very lazy, domestic servant. And if she doesn't get down to the family abode soon and cope with the dust and dishes, I'll brain her. Not," he added as he departed, "that she has a brain to be brained."

Both of the girls listened until his heavy, angry footsteps died away. Then Trixie whirled on Honey. "Now you've done it. No matter what I do or say, Mart will never take me seriously."

Honey tossed her light brown hair back from her slim shoulders. "Even if you live to be ninety, Trixie, Mart will never take seriously anything you do or say. You might as well face that, here and now, and let him in on the scheme. What I mean is, he adores Brian even more than you do, so he *will* take seriously the whole business about the diamond ring."

"Never," Trixie said defiantly. "Don't forget that I've lived with Mart ever since I was born. He just wouldn't cooperate, although he might try. He'd laugh his head off at all the wrong moments. Not," she added as she started for the door, "that he has a head to be laughed off."

Honey hastily followed her out into the hall, and they clung to each other there for a minute, laughing almost hysterically.

"Oh, all right," Honey finally gulped. "*Don't* let Mart in on the secret. But mark you my words, O Lily Maid of Astolat, you'll live to rue the day."

Trixie said nothing, but as she hurried home, she couldn't help shivering a little. Not so much because it was a cold, crisp fall day, but because she felt in her bones that Honey was right. Every time that she, Trixie, had tried to solve a problem without consulting Mart, they had always ended up in a near-catastrophe because, as it turned out, they had both been working along the same lines but at cross-purposes with each other.

In the warm kitchen at home, Trixie plunged her cold hands into the sinkful of hot, sudsy water. Pretty soon she would have to go upstairs and don a dainty frock. The very thought made her shiver again.

Her parents and Brian would certainly look at her with expressions that meant that they thought she had lost her mind. Bobby, of course, wouldn't notice. It would be all the same to him if she appeared in a gunnysack or a ball gown with a long train.

Mart, however, was something else again. He would not only look at her askance if she dressed for dinner, but he would make caustic remarks.

"Oh, nuts," Trixie reflected. "Honey's probably right. I should let Mart in on the secret. But I can't. There are so many problems involved. He'd be sure to let the cat out of the bag, and Brian would know why I wanted that silly old diamond ring. And if Brian knew, he'd never let me ask Dad to take it out of the bank."

Glamour Girl • 6

It was agony, but Trixie somehow did it. She appeared at dinner that evening wearing a dainty red-and-white polka-dotted party dress and her new black patent leather slippers. She had brushed and dampened her blond curls so that they looked almost as neat as though they had been set by a beauty parlor expert. She had also helped herself to her mother's hand lotion and toilet water.

The whole thing had been such an effort that she found she couldn't walk naturally. Instead of racing over to the table and sliding into her chair, she moved as stiffly as though she were a puppet controlled by strings.

A feminine Pinocchio, that's just what I am, she reflected grimly as she marched up to the table and sat down.

Nobody said a word for a long minute. Then, as though they, too, were controlled by strings, Trixie's father and brothers all, simultaneously, took large sips from their water tumblers. Then Mr. Belden patted his small moustache with his napkin and carefully cleared his throat.

"Good evening, *Miss* Belden," he said in a voice that Trixie had never heard him use before. He sounded as though he were choking in spite of the water he had gulped. He coughed again. "Haven't you made a mistake? Our Thanksgiving party does not take place until a week from next Thursday. The twenty-sixth, to be exact, and according to my calendar, today is only the sixteenth."

"Oh, Dad." Trixie waved her hands airily and wished that her fingernails were not so stubby. "How *can* you be so ridic? This isn't a party dress. It's just a very simple little thing Moms found last summer in a bargain basement. But it *is* becoming, isn't it? I mean, Ben liked it." She stared down at her plate and was sorry that she hadn't had time to put mascara on her sandy eyelashes. "Of course, it does need jewelry to set it off. Don't you agree? Just a simple little pin or a necklace or a ring would do it."

Mart uttered a sound that was identical with the yelp that Reddy emitted whenever Bobby accidentally stepped on his tail. He drained his water glass and wordlessly took it over to the sink. Mrs. Belden turned around from the counter at that exact moment, and they almost collided. She was carrying a large platter of fried chicken, and she set it down on the table mat in front of her husband's plate. Then she turned and stared at Trixie with a quizzical expression on her youthful, pretty face.

"My, honey," she said, "you look nice. I'm so glad you like that dress. But, Trixie, dear, jewelry would ruin the effect. Perhaps that strand of seed pearls your Aunt Alicia gave you last Christmas, but nothing else. Where *is* that necklace, Trixie?"

Trixie gulped both air and water. She hadn't the faintest idea of where that seed-pearl necklace was. The fact that she had lost it almost immediately after she received it was one of the reasons why her father had insisted upon putting her diamond ring in the safe-deposit box.

Brian spoke up then. "I know where that necklace is," he said coldly. "Bobby planted it in the garden last spring so he could grow some pearl bushes. He planted it seed pearl by seed pearl, didn't you, Bobby?"

Bobby did not deign to reply. He wrinkled his nose at Trixie and said, "You smell funny. Mostly, you smell all nice and sunshiny the way Reddy does after he's gone swiming in the lake. Now you smell sort of—"

Mart came back to the table with his glass then and said, "We know, Bobby. None of us will ever forget the day you got the flea powder can mixed up with Moms's talcum powder. Reddy will never forget it, either." He stopped behind Trixie's chair and sniffed elaborately. "Yes, Bobby, you're quite right. She does smell very much the way Reddy did on that unfortunate occasion."

Trixie, although consumed with the desire to throw a plate at Mart, mentally counted to ten. " 'A rose by any other name would smell as sweet,' " she quoted from *Romeo and Juliet.*

Mart groaned and said to Brian, "She's gone in for non sequiturs in a big way, no?"

"Yes," Brian said succinctly.

Trixie ignored them. "The point is," she said sweetly, "since I haven't got a seed-pearl necklace, I simply must have that diamond ring Jim gave me. Please, Dad, won't you get it out of the bank? I mean, Ben is the sophisticated type of boy who expects his date to be at least dressed." She turned to her mother. "Honestly, Moms, I feel positively naked in this dress without any jewelry."

Mrs. Belden hastily went to the refrigerator and came back with a large wooden bowl of tossed green salad. "Yes, Trixie," she said in a strange voice, "you're quite right. That ring is yours; you earned it, and if you really want to wear it while Ben Riker is visiting the Wheelers during the Thanksgiving holidays, there is no reason why you shouldn't. That is, of course, if your father has no objections."

Trixie's father, who was serving the fried chicken, said nothing. He merely nodded, but Brian folded his arms and cleared his throat.

"Well, I have some objections," he said staunchly. "Ben Riker is a creep of the first water. Because he goes to a private boarding school, his vacation begins next weekend. It's going to be bad enough to have him and his practical jokes interfering with our work on the clubhouse. But if Trixie is going to swoon around flashing diamond rings in that goon's face, well, I—I quit!"

Trixie clenched her fists in her lap, yearning to say, "Oh, Brian, I'm only doing it for your sake. I despise Ben Riker as much as you do." Aloud, she finally managed to say, "Naturally, Brian, because you and Mart are so uncouth, you don't appreciate Ben. He is, well, I might as well confess it—my very own ideal."

Mart emitted another feeble yelp, and then silence reigned again. They were all looking at Trixie with expressions on their faces that said plainly that they thought she had lost her mind. All of them except Bobby, who was one of the few young people who had never been a victim of Ben's practical jokes. "I 'dore Ben," Bobby said complacently. "He's one of my very best friends. He holps me catch frogs."

Mart said to Brian in a loud aside. "He sure does. And what does he do with said frogs? He puts 'em in the cook's bed. So the cook leaves, and Miss Trask has to cope until she can lure another one out to the Manor House. Oh, fine! Ben is *such* a jolly fellow!"

"Oh, veddy, veddy jolly," Brian agreed in a very British tone of voice. "What ho, and all that sort of thing."

"I like crab apple jolly," Bobby announced. "And so does Ben."

"That's just it," Mrs. Belden said hastily. "Ben is really a very nice boy." She reached over to pat Trixie's hand. "A very nice boy. He's just young for his age, that's all."

"So is Trixie," Brian said in a very older-brother tone of voice. "For *her* age, I mean. And just because she's temporarily insane, Dad, doesn't mean you should let her have that diamond ring so Bobby can plant it under a barberry bush."

It went on like that all week. Trixie, acting on advice she received from Di Lynch and Honey, did everything possible to convince her parents that she was now ladylike enough to wear the ring Jim had given her. She wore sloppy clothes only when she exercised the horses and did her chores. She wrote *Trixie Belden loves Benjamin Riker* on scraps of paper and left them in strategic spots all over the house. Di and Honey donated to the cause all kinds of costume jewelry, which Trixie wore every evening at dinner. By Thursday night, Brian and Mart, worn out by the work they had to do on the clubhouse during the few hours of daylight after school, stopped making comments. She appeared at the table wearing six bracelets on each arm, earrings, and ropes of cheap pearls around her neck. Nobody, not even Bobby, said a word. Trixie sank into her chair and said dramatically, "My hands—they feel so naked. If only I had just one teeny-weeny diamond ring."

Mr. Belden groaned. "Very well, Trixie," he said. "I'll bring your ring home from the bank tomorrow afternoon. You may keep it until you go back to school on the Monday after Thanksgiving. Then *it* goes back into our safe-deposit box. Do you understand?"

Trixie jumped up and raced around the table to throw her arms around her father. "Oh, Dad," she cried, "you don't know what this means to me. You'll never, *never* know."

Brian and Mart said tiredly to each other in unison, "Ugh! How *sed*imental can our sibling get?"

"She'll drop that ring down the kitchen drain first time she washes a dish," Brian predicted.

"I don't think so," Mart argued. "She'll lose it in the chicken-feed bin, with all that entails. *We* will have to sift the grain and mash in order to retrieve it."

"Oh, I doubt that," Brian said sarcastically. "Too easy, much too simple. She'll wear it when she goes swimming in the lake, and then we'll have to use grappling irons, or maybe drain the lake. That would mean damming up all the brooks and streams around here. But Trixie wouldn't care. What's a few thousand dead fish to a girl's whim?"

Bobby chimed in, beating on his plate with a spoon to attract attention. "You better not lose that ring, Trixie. It must be worth a zillion dollars."

Trixie ignored them all. She had won the battle. On Saturday morning, when she and Honey exercised the horses, they would ride to Mr. Lytell's little store. She would give him the ring as security so then he would have no excuse for selling Brian's jalopy.

Suspicions • 7

IT'S NOT AS SIMPLE as you think," Honey argued on Saturday morning as they trotted their horses through the woods on the north side of Glen Road. "You've got your ring, yes, but you know how peculiar Mr. Lytell is. He's an old gossip, and he's always very suspicious, even when there's nothing to be suspicious about. What makes you think he won't tell your father that you gave him the ring as security for Brian's jalopy?" She reined in Strawberry because just ahead of them on the narrow path was a fallen tree. "Now what?" she demanded over her shoulder.

Trixie, who was riding Mrs. Wheeler's gentle little

mare, Lady, stopped, too. "Umm," Trixie said, peering at the debris. "I guess we'll have to get off, tie our horses to a tree, and move that stuff, Honey."

"We can't," Honey wailed. "We're not strong enough. It would take a bulldozer, Trixie Belden, and you know it."

"I thought a bulldozer had already cleared all of these paths," Trixie said. "Isn't this part of your father's game preserve, Honey?"

Honey nodded. "I guess the crew Regan hired skipped this path. We'll have to go back to the fork and take the other one. This is just a shortcut to Mr. Lytell's land, you know."

"Umm," Trixie said again. "Shortcut is right. That other trail winds all over the place. It's absolutely, positively labyrinthine, as Mart would say. We'll be sure to get lost, Honey. You know how dumb we both are about where the points of the compass are."

Honey giggled. "Jim says we were both born without a sense of direction. Maybe we'd better go back to Glen Road and ride to Mr. Lytell's store that way. It's much longer, and we can only walk the horses, but it'll probably save time in the end."

"No," Trixie said soberly. "Let's don't do that. Let's make up our minds that we *won't* get lost. I have a feeling that pretty soon it's going to be important for us to know how to find our way around your father's game preserve." She turned Lady around and started back toward the fork.

Honey followed suit with Strawberry. "I don't know what you mean, Trixie," she complained. "Why should we worry about this labyrinth? Even if we knew how to shoot a gun, we'd never kill any kind of bird, and certainly not a deer."

"You can't shoot deer with a gun," Trixie informed her. "It's against the law in Westchester County. You have to use a longbow. The laws are very strict. This year, for instance, you can only hunt deer during the last two weeks in November and the first two weeks in December."

"I didn't know that," Honey admitted. "But what difference does it make? Why should we care? The only longbows I ever saw were pictures of them in *Robin Hood* and books like that."

"Don't be silly," Trixie said. "Your father must have a longbow. Otherwise, why did he stock his preserve with deer and have Fleagle build feeding stations for them and all?"

"I don't think Daddy knew about the laws when he stocked the preserve," Honey said. "Anyway, he won't be able to do much hunting this year because he's not returning until a week from tomorrow, which is the twenty-ninth of the month." They had reached the fork now and stopped their horses. "The path on your left," Honey said, "*I* think goes west, and we want to go east, don't we?"

"Do we?" Trixie asked. "Yes, we do." She answered her own question. "The sun rises in the east, and I've often seen it coming up behind that stand of pines next to Mr. Lytell's store. Anyway, the path on my left is only a path and probably doesn't lead anywhere. What we want to do is follow the *trails*."

"I don't know how you can tell the difference," Honey said. "They all look the same to me. But, as Mart would say, by the process of elimination, if one of these things is a path, then the other one must be a trail. So let's go." She nudged Strawberry into a trot and led the way eastward. Over her shoulder she said, "I wish you wouldn't be so mysterious, Trixie. Why do you think we should try to solve the mystery of this labyrinth?"

"Because," Trixie said, "this weekend we've got to talk Miss Trask and Regan into letting us have the gamekeeper's job. Nobody's answered the ads they've put into all the newspapers. And we've just got to earn fifty dollars during the next week. If we don't, how can I get my ring from Mr. Lytell so Dad can put it back into the bank on the Monday after Thanksgiving?"

"Oh, no," Honey moaned. "It's all so complicated. You haven't even *given* the ring to Mr. Lytell yet, and now you're worrying about getting it back." She chuckled. "Aren't you sort of putting the cart before the horse? Or should I say, the ring before the jalopy? Oh, *oh!* What *am* I trying to say?"

"Whatever it is," Trixie chortled, "it makes no sense. The problem is this: I *have* to make Mr. Lytell accept the ring today, and I have to get it back a week from tomorrow. So we *have* to get the gamekeeper's job so we'll have fifty dollars by next Saturday."

They had reached a small clearing now and were riding abreast instead of single file. "You're right," Honey cried enthusiastically. "But we've got to sell Regan on the idea. The trouble is that the boys won't be able to help us much. They're too busy fixing up the clubhouse."

"That's the point," Trixie agreed. "So it's up to us, Honey. We can patrol the preserve just as well as the boys, so long as we don't get lost every single time we go into it."

"I'm lost right now," Honey said with a nervous laugh. "This clearing doesn't look familiar."

"They look different in the fall," Trixie said, feeling a little nervous herself. "I mean, we might have had a picnic here last summer but wouldn't recognize the same spot now."

"I really wish we'd left behind a bottle or something," Honey said. "Any kind of bottle with a map or a compass in it would come in handy now. There are three paths leading out of this clearing, Trixie.

Which one shall we take? Or is one of them a trail? What *is* the difference, anyway? I know Indians used to blaze trails by leaving all sorts of signs on trees, but there haven't been any Indians around here for ages."

"Somebody's been around here recently," Trixie said as she swung out of the saddle. "And whoever it was couldn't have been Fleagle, because he left Sunday night before it rained." She pointed to a large footprint in the small section of the clearing where there were no pine needles. "It wasn't an Indian, either. It was somebody who was wearing hunting boots, and since all of this property is posted, he was trespassing." She lowered her voice to a whisper. "In other words, Honey Wheeler, that footprint probably belongs to a *poacher!*"

Honey sighed. "I don't think that footprints belong to people. I mean, after all, you leave them behind and don't feel possessive about them. Anyway, that footprint probably belongs to Mr. Lytell, and I'm very glad to see it, because it must mean that we're very near his store."

"Don't be silly," Trixie cried. "Mr. Lytell's not a poacher."

"I didn't say he was," Honey said with another sigh. "Oh, why must you always be such a detective, Trixie? Mr. Lytell is a nosy old gossip, but he wouldn't harm a fly. So you just can't call him a poacher. Besides, I don't think there *are* any poachers anymore. They only lived in very olden times in England. And even then, like Robin Hood, they were very good things. The kings had no business not letting their starving subjects kill deer."

It was Trixie's turn to sigh. "I've got news for you, Honey," she said as she climbed back into the saddle. "There *are* such things as poachers nowadays. That's why the state of New York hires wardens, whom they call game protectors. That's one reason why your father has to have a gamekeeper. A poacher is a person who breaks the game laws, and he is also anybody who, although he may not be breaking a game law, kills or catches any living thing on somebody else's property."

"Oh," Honey said in a subdued tone of voice. "Well, I guess that settles it. If there are poachers lurking around, you and I can't be gamekeepers. What would we do even if we did catch a poacher poaching?"

"Why, that's simple," Trixie replied. "We'd simply track him to his lair. And if he didn't have a lair, he'd have a car or a truck or something so he could tote away the carcasses of everything he'd illegally killed. In that case, all we'd have to do is to get the registration number of his car and then report him to the police."

Honey shuddered. "*You* may think it's simple,

but the very word, carcass, makes me feel like fainting. You know perfectly well, Trixie Belden, that I always faint at the sight of blood."

Trixie grinned impishly. "You know perfectly well, Honey Wheeler, that you got over that phobia a long time ago. You're not any more afraid of poachers and carcasses than I am. Anyway, let's continue along the trail. It's always the widest one of the paths, so this must be it."

"It's not the one the toe of that print is pointing to," Honey objected. "I'm sure it isn't."

"That doesn't mean anything," Trixie said, leading the way along the trail. "A poacher, unless he was traveling on horseback, wouldn't stick to the trails. He'd sneak along the paths."

Honey was silent for a few minutes while Strawberry trotted along behind Lady. Then she said, "I think that footprint was left by Mr. Lytell. He trespasses on Daddy's game preserve all the time, but nobody minds. I mean, he has to when he goes out riding on that old gray mare of his. But I'm sure he doesn't do any poaching."

"I'm sure of that, too," Trixie said. "I'm also sure he didn't leave the footprint. Because he never wears hunting boots."

"Oh, all right," Honey said grimly. "There is a poacher. So we'd better tell the boys right away."

"Heavens, no!" Trixie cried. "They'd only make

fun of me. You know how they are, never suspicious of anything unless a crime is committed practically under their noses." She pulled Lady to a walk as they approached the macadam road. On the other side of it was Mr. Lytell's little store.

"I'll wait here for you," Honey offered, "and hold Lady's reins. But hurry, Trixie, please."

"Okay," Trixie said and swung out of the saddle. Just then a man she had never seen before came out of the store. He was tall and gaunt with broad, slightly stooping shoulders. The visor of his red cap hid most of his weather-beaten face, but Trixie could see enough of his features to be positive that he was a stranger. The very costume he was wearing was proof enough of that. Most of Mr. Lytell's customers were neighbors whom she had known ever since she was a little girl, and even at masquerades they never wore such quaint garments.

"My grandfather," she whispered to Honey, "wore a turtleneck sweater like that when he played football in high school. There's a photo of him with his team in an old album at home. And he wore funny-looking knickers like those when he played golf. But they were white linen, not khaki wool."

The man, who was carrying a large cardboard carton under one arm, paid no attention to them as he entered the woods and disappeared from view almost immediately.

"There must be a path there," Honey said in a low voice. "But I never would have noticed it, would you?"

Trixie investigated. "There is a path, but nobody except a mouse or a rabbit would call it one." Consumed with curiosity, she raced across the road and into the overcrowded store. Mr. Lytell was adding coal to the fire in his potbellied stove, so Trixie had to shout to get his attention.

"Who was that man who just left here?"

Mr. Lytell straightened and turned to face her with a petulant frown. "Trixie Belden," he snapped. "What do you mean by rushing in here and yelling at me as though I were stone-deaf? It's high time you ceased being such a harum-scarum tomboy. I've a good mind to pick up the phone and call your mother. There *is* a real lady, and if you didn't look so much like her, I'd never believe that you were her daughter."

Trixie suppressed a sigh. Mr. Lytell had said this kind of thing about her so many times before that it was boring to listen. She knew perfectly well that he did not approve of her, so she began to worry for fear he would not accept the diamond ring. Too late, she realized that if Honey had offered it to him as security for Brian's jalopy, there wouldn't have been any trouble. Mr. Lytell *did* approve of Honey, and the fact that her parents were so rich would have kept him from becoming suspicious. But now all she could do was plunge into the situation and hope for the best.

She took the tiny jewel case from the pocket of her jeans and put it on the counter. "Sorry I was so noisy, Mr. Lytell," she said contritely. "But I was curious because I never saw that man before. Anyway, this is why I came to see you." With a flick of her fingernail, she snapped open the gold clasp of the case. Even in that musty, dusty store, the facets of the diamond glittered.

The storekeeper uttered a sound that made Trixie think of a billy goat's bleat. As a matter of fact, the storekeeper, with his wispy moustache, did look rather like a goat. She suddenly felt as though she were taking part in a scene from *Through the Looking Glass*. The storekeeper in that scene had been a sheep, but she *had* been wearing glasses, and the sheep's store was as cluttered as this one. For a moment, while she tried to keep from laughing, Trixie was sure that Mr. Lytell would grab a pair of needles and begin to knit.

Instead, he grabbed the ring from the jewel case and brought it over to the strong light above the desk in the back of the store. Trixie followed him, not daring to say a word. After what seemed like hours, he turned and said in an awed tone of voice, "This diamond ring is worth about two hundred dollars. *Where did you get it, Trixie Belden?*"

"Jim Frayne gave it to me ages ago," Trixie said. "It was his great-aunt's, and because I found it before the old Mansion burned to the ground, Jim felt that it belonged to me." In a rush of words she went on: "You remember, Mr. Lytell, when old Mr. Frayne's house burned. And how Jim ran away afterward and all. You've just got to believe me. The ring *is* mine. But I want you to have it."

"Me?" He swiveled his chair around to glare at her. "You've never made much sense in your life, Trixie Belden, but now you're making no sense at all. Why on earth should you give me this ring?"

Trixie took a deep breath and, because her knees felt so weak, hoisted herself onto the counter. "Because of Brian," she finally got out. "I mean his jalopy. I mean *your* jalopy, but it's really Brian's, except that he hasn't got the fifty dollars anymore. On account of the storm and what the blue spruce did to our clubhouse, you know. I—"

"No, I don't know," Mr. Lytell exploded, and he didn't sound at all like a sheep or a goat now. He sounded more like an angry bull. Then he lowered his voice and said, as though he were speaking to a backward kindergarten child, "Let's start at the beginning. Brian wanted to buy my old Ford. He didn't have enough money, but because I like Brian, I cooperated so that he could get the license plates and take out the insurance. In other words, I gave him the car with the understanding that he would give me the fifty dollars today. He called me day before yesterday to say that he could not produce fifty dollars, after all. So I am going to turn the car over to a secondhand dealer this afternoon."

"Yes, yes," Trixie cried nervously. "I mean, no, NO! That's just the point. You've hit the nail on the thumb, Mr. Lytell. How smart you are. You understand now, about the diamond and all, don't you?"

He pushed his eyeglasses farther up the bridge of his nose. "I don't understand one word that you're talking about, Trixie Belden." Then just when Trixie thought it was all hopeless, a smile crinkled his face. He picked up the diamond again and said in a whisper, "Yes, I do understand now. You're giving me this as security so that Brian will be able to have my old Ford, after all."

Trixie nodded her head up and down vehemently. Because he was whispering, she felt that she had to whisper, too. "But you mustn't let Brian know. He gave us the fifty dollars he should have given to you this morning. So we could repair the clubhouse. But the money really belongs to him. I mean to you. I mean, the jalopy should really be Brian's." Her voice dwindled away into a rasping cough. Mr. Lytell had that suspicious look on his face again.

"If you boys and girls needed money," he said,

"why didn't you sell this ring, Trixie? I'm not a pawnbroker." He closed the jewel case and snapped the clasp back in place. "There's something fishy about all this. I don't like it. I just don't like it."

"But I don't want to sell it," Trixie wailed in despair. "Oh, Mr. Lytell, I know you don't like me, but you do like Brian. Please try to understand. We're all going to work hard so we can earn the money and pay Brian back just as soon as we can. Maybe by this time next week we'll have fifty dollars. Then you can give Brian his car and give me back my ring."

For answer, he got up slowly, went over to his safe, twirled the dial, opened the door, and put the jewel case inside. "Miss Trask," he mumbled to himself, "thinks the world of you, and I think the world of Miss Trask. So there must be some good in you." He was almost, but not quite, smiling.

"Very well, Trixie Belden," he said in a loud clear voice, "I'll keep the car and the ring here until next Saturday. If you don't produce fifty dollars by then, I'll—" He emphatically left the sentence unfinished, but Trixie knew what he meant. If she didn't redeem the ring within a week, he would have to report the whole transaction to her father.

"Thanks," she said weakly and somehow made her trembling legs carry her out to where Honey was waiting with the horses.

A Job for the Bob-Whites • 8

WELL," HONEY promptly demanded, "how did you make out?"

Trixie gathered the reins and mounted Lady. "We're safe for another week," she said. "So now we've just got to get that gamekeeper's job."

Honey nodded. "Was Mr. Lytell very suspicious?"

"He couldn't have been more suspicious," Trixie replied, "if he'd caught me stealing the ring from Moms's jewelry box. I'm sure that's who—whom—he thinks it belongs to."

"Naturally," Honey said. "Mr. Lytell wouldn't give anybody anything, so he couldn't possibly believe that Jim gave you that ring. I'm really surprised he kept it as security."

"It's all due to Miss Trask," Trixie said weakly. "Mr. Lytell thinks she's just wonderful, you know, and I gather she's told him she likes me, in spite of all my faults."

Honey giggled. "Everybody likes you, Trixie, and you really haven't got any bad faults. But isn't it funny how Miss Trask and Regan are forever getting us out of scrapes?"

"Let's hope they don't stop now," Trixie said as they cantered along the trail. "They've just got to give us the gamekeeper's job, starting tomorrow morning, so we can earn fifty dollars by this time next weekend."

"We'll talk to Regan about it first," Honey agreed, "while we're grooming the horses and cleaning the tack."

When the trail narrowed, they trotted single file, and Trixie said, "I wonder who that strange man was."

"Didn't you ask Mr. Lytell?" Honey demanded. "As a matter of fact, you did ask him. I heard you yell at the top of your lungs, 'Who was that man who just left here?' "

Trixie chuckled ruefully. "That was the trouble. I shouted, and Mr. Lytell got mad. Said I was a harum-scarum tomboy and all that sort of thing. So I didn't dare ask him again."

"Well, it really doesn't matter," Honey said, without much interest. "We'll probably never see that man again."

"It does matter," Trixie argued. "I think he's a poacher."

Honey laughed. "You've got poachers on the brain, Trixie. Mart would say that you had poached brains instead of scrambled brains."

"Don't mention Mart's name to me," Trixie begged. "What I've been through this week! He and Brian teased me so much I almost gave up. It was simply torture getting dressed for dinner every evening and having to sit there and listen to their wisecracks."

"Never mind," Honey said soothingly. "You succeeded, and it will all turn out to have been worth it in the end. This week has been awful for everybody. Miss Trask is worn out with trying to do both Celia's and Tom's work, and sometimes she's almost cross, if you can believe it."

"I can't," Trixie replied. "She's always so nice and cheery. And that reminds me. Did you hear anything from the honeymooners? Moms was worried the night of the storm because trees were crashing down on the highways upstate. I didn't worry, because Tom is such a marvelous driver. I figured they had sense enough to stop off at an inn until the storm ended."

"They did," Honey told her. "They're in Canada now. We all got postcards from them yesterday. They'll be back next weekend, thank goodness. When Mother called up from Florida on Wednesday, she told Miss Trask to hire a temporary maid and a temporary chauffeur at any price, but Miss Trask said it wouldn't be worthwhile breaking them in for such a short time. She has enough trouble breaking in cooks, who are forever leaving."

"I hope for Miss Trask's sake," Trixie said, "that Ben Riker doesn't try to put any frogs in this cook's bed."

"That would be the straw that broke the camel's back," Honey agreed. "If the cook left while Celia and Tom are away, I think Miss Trask would probably quit, too."

"And that," Trixie added, "would be the end. She's just wonderful. Oh, Honey, let's canter. I can't wait to find out if Miss Trask and Regan will give us the gamekeeper's job."

"I can't, either," Honey admitted. "If we can win Regan over to our side, I'm sure Miss Trask will agree. But Regan can be stubborn at times. We'll have to be careful, and also we had better be very sure that we do a perfect job when we groom the horses."

Half an hour later, Honey began the conversation with Regan: "Oh, about those ads you and Miss

Trask put in the papers. Did anybody apply for the gamekeeper's job?"

Trixie couldn't help grinning. Honey was trying so hard to make her voice sound casual as she worked on Strawberry with a currycomb.

"No," Regan replied from the doorway of the tack room. "And, in my opinion, nobody ever will. There aren't many people left who can afford game preserves, and they've got all the gamekeepers there are left working for them."

"Oh," Honey said as she led Strawberry back to his stall. "Do you have to be so very wonderful to be a gamekeeper? I didn't think much of Fleagle. I mean, I thought he was really sort of dumb, didn't you?"

Trixie's secret grin widened. There just wasn't anybody in the world as tactful as Honey Wheeler.

"Fleagle," Regan said in a wrathful tone of voice, "was as stupid as they come. Why, even you and Trixie know more about horses than he does."

"That's just what I thought," Honey said innocently. "Trixie and I, working early in the morning and after school, could be just as good a gamekeeper as Fleagle was, couldn't we? I mean, what is there to do except ride along the trails and sort of patrol? Trixie and I were riding along the trails on this side of the road only this morning, and we didn't get lost once."

Regan placed his big freckled hands on his hips. "No kiddin'?" he demanded. "Now, that's a record, isn't it?" Grinning broadly, he added, "I suppose you captured, single-handedly, a whole army of poachers, too."

"Oh, don't tease us, please, Regan," Honey begged. "We Bob-Whites have just got to get that job. On account of the clubhouse and Brian's jalopy, you know. And you know perfectly well there aren't any poachers, and if there were, the boys could capture them, single-handedly and all."

Regan guffawed. "The boys can single-handedly go out and repair the feeding stations that were knocked down by the wind. One thing is sure: *I* certainly haven't got the time to do it."

"That's just the point," Trixie put in. "The boys are very good at repairs. They'll do all that sort of thing. Honey and I, while we're patrolling, can scatter grain around for the birds and whatever it is that deer like. After all, Regan, I've been feeding our chickens for years. There's not much difference between a chicken and a pheasant when you get right down to it. Or a partridge, either. At one time they were all eggs, you know."

Regan howled with laughter. Then he sobered. "You girls have got something there. All five of you kids working together could certainly do as good a job as that Fleagle did, and cause me a lot less trouble." He started for the stable door. "I'm going right in and talk to Miss Trask about it."

When he had gone, Honey and Trixie collapsed on the floor of the tack room. "Keep your fingers crossed," Honey said. "Miss Trask is very understanding and all, but she just might not go for the idea."

Trixie giggled. "I can't keep my fingers crossed and clean my saddle and bridle."

"Well, cross your toes, then," Honey retorted, handing her a sponge and a can of saddle soap. "This tack has got to be super-perfect today of all days."

They worked in silence until they had cleaned and put away every bit of the leather. Then they hurried outside and down to the clubhouse. The boys had finished rebuilding the wall and were now working on the roof.

Mart, sitting astride the ridgepole, called down to the girls, "Hi, you lazy females."

"Lazy, indeed," Trixie yelled back. "We just finished exercising all of the horses and cleaning about five million tons of leather."

"Oh, don't you and Mart start arguing," Honey begged. "When you two get going, you go on forever." She tilted back her pretty face and called up to Jim, who was hammering shingles into place. "Jim! Can't you boys quit for a while so we can hold an emergency meeting? Something important's happened. I mean, about to happen. At least, I hope it'll happen."

Jim removed the nails from his mouth and stared down at her. "Gleeps, Honey! Can't you ever make a simple sentence without tacking on a lot of 'I thinks' and 'I means'?"

"No, she can't," Brian answered the question as he started down the ladder. "She's been exposed to Trixie too long. The habit is as catching as measles."

"I've got news for you, Jim," Mart added as he followed Brian down the ladder. "Neither one of them ever makes sense. Lovely girls, and all that, at least, Honey is, but—"

"Now who's 'at-leasting'?" Trixie demanded.

Jim slid down the roof and, grasping the gutter for a second, swung himself to the ground. Trixie couldn't help giving him an admiring glance. All of the boys were strong and supple, but Jim was the most athletic one of them all. There really wasn't anything worth doing that Jim couldn't do—and do awfully well.

Without realizing that she was thinking out loud, she said to him, "You're just as good a gamekeeper as Fleagle was, if not better."

Jim reached out and gave one of her sandy curls a gentle tug. "I'm going to have a great big, scarlet ribbon made for you, and on it, printed in gold, will be 'Miss Nonsense of America.' "

"Yes, yes," Mart agreed. "I'll be her press agent. We'll tour the country together, I in my limousine and she in her cage. Remind me to make a sign for that cage, Jim. Something to the effect that customers should not poke their fingers through the bars unless they wish to lose said fingers."

Trixie bared her teeth at him. "I wish I were a lioness so I could bite your head off."

"Oh, please," Honey implored them. "Let's go into what's left of the clubhouse and hold a meeting." She led the way, and when they had gathered around the table, she said, "Trixie and I were just talking to Regan about our maybe getting the gamekeeper job, at least for a week, anyway. He's talking to Miss Trask about it now."

There was silence for a minute; then Mart emitted a loud, "WOW! If Miss Trask agrees, that's a sure fifty bucks." He turned to Brian. "Maybe you can get your jalopy, after all."

Brian shook his head. "That Ford's at the second-hand car dealer's place now. That is, if it hasn't already been sold."

"Well, let's not worry about that now," Trixie said hastily. "The important thing is for somebody to talk Miss Trask into agreeing with Regan that we should have the job." She pointed her finger at Jim. "You're that somebody."

"That's right," Brian agreed. "And I now understand what Trixie was driving at when she said you'd make a good gamekeeper. If you didn't have to go to school every day, Jim, you could hold down the job all by yourself."

"Single-handedly is the word," Honey said with a giggle. "It's one of Regan's favorites. He keeps on using it the way Trixie and I keep saying—"

"Never mind," Jim interrupted. "If Regan's on our side, we've practically won the battle. But I'll go up to the house now and see what's cooking." He hurried off.

They sat there, tensely waiting, until he came back in less than ten minutes. There was a broad grin on his freckled face, and he greeted them all with a loud whoop.

"It's all set—except for a slight hitch."

"Oh, no," Honey moaned. "Don't tell us. *We* know. Miss Trask doesn't think Trixie and I can cope with poachers."

He threw one arm around her slim shoulders and gave her a brotherly hug. "The chance of you and Trixie stumbling across a poacher is one in a million, little sister. So don't you two let your vivid imaginations run away with you while you patrol."

"Well, what *is* the slight hitch, then?" Trixie demanded. She found it hard to be patient.

Jim pointed to the gaping hole in the ceiling.

"That," he said succinctly. "We've got to stop working on the roof while we clear the paths and then repair the feeding stations."

"Oh, nuts," Mart cried. "That'll probably take the entire week, and in the meantime—"

"Oh, let's not be so pessimistic," Brian broke in cheerfully. "The paths may not be blocked. And how do we know? Maybe all of the feeding stations are still intact."

Jim shrugged. "In either case, we've got to get going at once. Let's just hope this bright, sunny weather lasts until we boys are through. The girls, of course, will have to do all of the patrolling. Until school closes next Wednesday for the Thanksgiving holidays, that means, Trixie and Honey, that you kids will have to get up at dawn. Can you do it?"

"Of course we can," Trixie retorted. "Tomorrow's Sunday, so we don't have to patrol early in the morning before school except on Monday, Tuesday, and Wednesday. Three days won't kill us."

"Says you," Mart put in. "You die a thousand deaths every morning when the alarm clock goes off at seven. Thus, according to my mental slide rule, you'll die two and a half thousand deaths when you have to get up at five-thirty."

"Oh, don't be so silly, Mart," Honey cried impatiently. "In the first place, your mental slide rule is all off. In the second place, Trixie and I *like* to ride early in the morning. After all, we've been doing it ever since the storm, because the horses simply have to be exercised, and you boys have been much too busy working on the roof of the clubhouse even to go near the stable."

"All right, all right," Jim said, grinning. "Then it's all settled. Except for one thing. When you girls patrol, for pete's sake, stick to the old bridle trails. Don't wander off on any of the paths. While we work, we'll cope with that part of the patrolling."

"Oh, heavens, yes," Mart cried. "By all means stick to the trails, ladies. Otherwise, we'll have to hire bloodhounds if we ever want to see you again." In a loud aside to Brian he added, "Not that we ever want to. Trixie, I mean. After all, Honey is handy with a needle, so it would be tragic if we lost *her*."

Jim chuckled. "But Trixie sort of grows on you. Now that I'm used to her form of insanity, I'd hate to lose her. She's sort of a human slide rule. Anybody who isn't as crazy as she is must be sane by comparison. If you see what I mean."

"We do; we do," Trixie said wearily. "Pardon me for moving around, but there's a shortage of strait-jackets. As soon as I can get into one, I'll curl up for a long winter's nap, while you heroes do all of my chores. Complete with Bobby and dawn patrol."

"Oh, no," Mart yelled. "Dawn patrol I could endure for the sake of the club. But Bobby, no. Why, if I had to do your Bobby-sitting for you, I'd be as crazy as you are in no time at all." He clenched his fist and tapped her lightly on the chin. "So *don't* go out and get lost!"

A Terrifying Scene • 9

SUNDAY TURNED out to be another crisp, cool, sunshiny day. Trixie and Honey met at the stable right after breakfast. As they saddled and bridled their horses, Honey said, "The boys sure did a lot of work yesterday afternoon. They cleared all of the paths, and Jim said this morning that he's not very worried about the feeding stations. All of the ones they inspected yesterday were all right."

"That's good," Trixie said as she swung up on the back of the lovely young mare, Susie. This horse theoretically belonged to Miss Trask, but because Miss Trask seldom had time to ride, Trixie felt that Susie really belonged to her.

Honey mounted Starlight and said, "This good weather can't last long, Trixie. And if the boys can't repair the clubhouse roof before we get sleet and snow and all, well, we might just as well forget that we ever had a clubhouse." They trotted along the path that led up to the section of the game preserve that lay behind the *Robin.* As they passed the red trailer, Honey said, "I'm *so* glad the honeymoon cottage escaped the storm. Celia and Tom would be brokenhearted if they came back and found the *Robin* the mess our clubhouse is. Oh, Trixie," she finished in a wail of despair, "I know I'm silly to get so upset, but all of my life, while I was going to boarding schools and camps, I kept dreaming about someday belonging to a boys' and girls' club—and—and now our clubhouse is ruined."

Trixie said nothing for a while. She knew that Honey, who had been a poor little rich girl until the Wheelers bought the Manor House and adopted Jim, would suffer more than any of the others if the clubhouse couldn't be rebuilt. And the funny part of it was that if Honey wanted a brand-new wonderful clubhouse, all she had to do was tell her father, and he would have one built for her right away. But none of the Bob-Whites, Honey least of all, would have liked that. So there was nothing to do but hope that the boys would have time to do the necessary work on the clubhouse roof before winter set in. The sky now, thank heavens, was a solid blue arch without a cloud in it. But you never could count on November weather. They might wake up on Thanksgving morning to find themselves in the midst of a blizzard.

"An ice storm," Honey was saying mournfully. "It could happen tonight or tomorrow night. And then, if it were followed by a high wind, why—"

"Oh, Honey," Trixie interrupted, "don't be such a Calamity Jane. Maybe all of the feeding stations are okay, so the boys can go right back to work on the clubhouse. Let's explore and make sure for ourselves."

"Oh, no," Honey cried, reining the big chestnut gelding to an abrupt stop. "We promised the boys that we wouldn't ever leave the trails, Trixie."

"We didn't do anything of the kind," Trixie retorted. "They tried to make us promise. Remember? But we didn't. Oh," she interrupted herself, "I suddenly remembered something. We shouldn't be patrolling this part of the game preserve now. We should be farther east and closer to Glen Road. I told Dad we'd ride to Mr. Lytell's store and get the Sunday papers."

"But, Trixie," Honey wailed, "why did you promise to do such a silly thing? We simply haven't time. Miss Trask would have got your family's papers when she went to get ours, as you know very well."

"There was a method in my madness," Trixie said, leading the way down toward the road. "I want to find out more about that strange character we saw yesterday."

Honey laughed helplessly. "The Man with the Red Cap! You're convinced he's a poacher. Oh, Trix! Why must you always think like an amateur detective?"

Trixie joined in her laughter. "I suppose I am silly to suspect somebody who probably never killed so much as a fly on somebody else's property, but he *was* wearing hunting boots, Honey."

They walked their horses along the trail. "Was he?" Honey asked. "I didn't notice. I was so fascinated by that turtleneck sweater and those weird woolen knickers he was wearing!"

"He was wearing hunting boots, all right," Trixie told her. "And he left a footprint on that tiny path he disappeared into. If we were FBI men, we could lift that footprint and match it up with the other one we found at the fork."

"Well, we're not FBI men, or women, either, for that matter," Honey said. "And I don't think poachers look like that strange man did. They should wear green clothes so they can fade into the forest the way Robin Hood did. No poacher in his right mind would barge around wearing a bright red cap."

"Yes, he would," Trixie argued. "During the deer

season, everyone in his right mind wears a red cap so he won't be mistaken for a deer."

"We're not," Honey reminded her.

"We're riding horses," Trixie said. "Nobody could suspect us of being a deer."

"Or does," Honey said with a laugh. "Not even centauresses. Anyway, I still don't think that funny-looking man is a poacher. He wasn't carrying a gun, for one thing. All he was carrying was a box of groceries. Because I was on my horse when he passed us, I could see what was in the carton, and it couldn't have been more innocent. Tea, coffee, sugar, salt, tiny cans of condensed milk—things like that. His wife probably sent him shopping, and—"

"But he was trespassing," Trixie interrupted.

"Pooh," Honey said. "He was probably taking a shortcut home. There's no harm in that."

"But where *is* his home?" Trixie demanded. "I never saw him before, so he can't be a neighbor. And he certainly wasn't planning to carry that big carton for miles and miles."

"He and his family might have moved into the neighborhood recently," Honey pointed out.

"That's not possible," Trixie said emphatically. "Your father bought up all the land around here that was for sale, didn't he?"

Honey nodded. "But that man might be living in a rented house."

"There aren't any," Trixie said. "You know as well as I do, Honey, that there are only huge estates around here. The people who own them have been living there for generations. They wouldn't think of renting them. Even if they did, that odd-looking man couldn't afford to pay the rent they'd ask."

"I'm not so sure about that," Honey said. "Sometimes people do rent their big country places—if they're going abroad, for instance. And you ought to know better than to judge a book by its cover. I never saw Jim's great-uncle, but you did. There was a very rich man who looked and lived like a pauper."

"True," Trixie agreed. "Oh, dear," she interrupted herself. "Here come the dogs. I thought they were with the boys."

Reddy and Jim's springer spaniel, Patch, came bounding out of a narrow path onto the trail.

"Go home," Trixie and Honey yelled in unison, but the dogs only replied with joyous barks. They were obviously on the trail of something, and, after greeting the girls, they raced off.

"Good riddance," Trixie said. "We couldn't possibly track down a poacher with those two barging around and barking their heads off."

"They'd come in mighty handy if we got lost," Honey said. "Although I suppose if we gave the horses their heads, they'd take us back home."

"Not these two," Trixie replied. "Strawberry and

Jupiter and Lady would, but Starlight and Susie don't know any more about this labyrinth than we do. Nobody has ever ridden them along these particular trails."

"I still think horses have a sort of homing-pigeon instinct or something," Honey said, "but let's not take any chances of getting lost, unless we're riding Strawberry and Lady."

"We'll never get lost so long as we stick to the trails," Trixie said. "They all come out on the road eventually." A few minutes later they caught sight of the little Glen Road store, and she said, "I've been thinking, Honey. I'd better not go near Mr. Lytell. He'd be sure to ask me a lot of questions about the ring and all. Here's the money. You buy the papers and sort of casually ask him who that man was we saw yesterday."

"All right," Honey agreed as she dismounted and handed the reins to Trixie. When she came back, she said, "Mr. Lytell is really very nice at times. See? He rolled the papers and tied them together so they'd be easy to carry."

"Give them to me," Trixie said, reaching down for the bundle. "They're my problem. Now, who is that strange man?"

"His name is Maypenny," Honey said, swinging back into the saddle. "And, believe it or not, he's owned property around here for simply ages."

"That's not possible," Trixie said flatly. "I never saw him before."

"It's true, though," Honey replied. "Mr. Lytell says he's sort of a hermit. He buys things from the store a few times a year, but mostly he lives on his land, which isn't very far from here."

"Oh," Trixie said in a disappointed tone of voice. "That explains why I never even heard of him. Well, I guess he's not a poacher, after all." She added thoughtfully, "It's kind of funny I never saw his house, though. Where is it?"

"I have no idea," Honey said. "Mr. Lytell tried to tell me where it was, but you know how vague I am when it comes to understanding directions. He sort of pointed as he talked about Mr. Maypenny, but since we were inside the store, I couldn't tell whether he was pointing to the south or the east. The points of the compass are very different indoors from what they are outdoors."

Trixie giggled. "To us they are, but not to normal people. Anyway, it doesn't matter. The important thing is to find out who left that footprint in the clearing. Let's look at it when we reach the fork."

"I suppose," Honey said dubiously, "now that we're gamekeepers, that is important. But why don't we say that Mr. Maypenny left it, and let it go at that?"

"He couldn't have left it," Trixie argued. "If he

has property of his own around here, why would he bother to trespass on your father's property? Since he's a hermit, he obviously never leaves home unless he has to. Mr. Lytell is different. He keeps on thinking that ancient Belle of his must be exercised every day, rain or shine, so he just *has* to trespass on the bridle trails."

"All right," Honey said placidly. "Then Mr. Lytell left that footprint. You don't know for sure, Trixie Belden, that he doesn't own a pair of hunting boots. Just because you've never seen him stir more than a few steps, unless he's riding Belle or in a car, doesn't mean he can't ever take a walk in the woods. And if he does, which I'm sure he must, he'd wear boots on account of the copperheads around here. Boots are like those red hats. Nobody in his right mind would stroll through the woods without boots at any time of the year."

"Don't be silly," Trixie snapped. "As soon as the weather gets cold, the snakes start to hibernate."

"Well, poison ivy doesn't hibernate," Honey said. "That's reason enough to wear boots. Jim was telling me only yesterday that when he was a little boy, he got the worst attack of poison ivy he ever had, in *January!*"

"I did, too," Trixie admitted.

Honey shook with laughter. "When you were a little *boy*, Trixie?"

"A tomboy, then," Trixie replied with a grin. "Gosh, Honey, I don't see how I can possibly stand another whole week of behaving like a little lady."

"The worst has yet to come," Honey said, her hazel eyes twinkling. "Cousin Ben arrives this afternoon, and you've got to act as though he were your very own dream man."

"Nightmare is the word," Trixie said with a shudder. "That creep! I don't think I can even look at him without crossing my eyes."

Honey laughed so hard she almost fell off her horse. "Don't worry," she finally got out. "He doesn't like you any more than you like him, so when you swoon around and act as though you were crazy about him, he probably won't even notice. He'll just think you're *crazy*, if anything."

"I am crazy," Trixie said mournfully. "Totally insane. I should be in a straitjacket. Why do I go through all this for Brian, who never says a kind word to me? I'm beginning to get one of those sibling complexes."

"*What* complexes?" Honey asked in amazement. "You must mean *sibilant*, which is another word for hissing like a snake."

"That's *not* what I mean," Trixie retorted, "although I do feel like hissing like a snake at Brian when he makes remarks about me at dinner. I'm talking about *sibling*, which is another word for brothers and sisters. I read about it in Brian's book on psychology. I couldn't understand much of it, but I think a sibling complex is the same thing as brotherly love, or, as in my case, brotherly *hate.*"

They had reached the clearing at the fork, and Honey slid off her horse to collapse on the ground, almost hysterical with laughter. "You're suffering from both kinds of complexes," she gulped. "Oh, Trixie, you and your brothers are so wonderful. You all go around behaving as though you despise one another, and everyone knows that Brian and Mart and Bobby idolize you just as much as you adore them."

Trixie dismounted and handed the reins of both horses to Honey. "You and Jim do all right as siblings, too, although you haven't had as much practice as we Beldens. Just to show you what I mean, I'll bet when Brian gets that jalopy, he'll teach Mart and Bobby how to drive before he gives me one single, solitary lesson."

She knelt to examine the footprint, then straightened. "You hold the horses, Honey. I'm going to explore along this path. It must lead somewhere."

"To the very heart of the labyrinth," Honey said, still chuckling. "There you'll find the Minotaur, as Theseus did on the Isle of Crete in Greek mythology. I'll be your Ariadne, but since we haven't a spool of silken thread, this string tied around the newspapers will just have to do, I guess."

"Don't be silly," Trixie cried impatiently. "I'm not going to go far enough away to get lost." She darted off along the narrow path and, a few minutes later, found herself in another small clearing. There she came upon a scene that was so frightening she couldn't even scream. She just stood there, staring with horror, then turned and raced back to Honey.

Trouble! • 10

HONEY, *Honey!*" Trixie gasped. "The most awful thing has happened." She collapsed on her knees in the small clearing, shuddering and covering her face with her hands.

Honey hastily wound the horses' reins around her wrist and hugged Trixie with her free arm. "Oh, Trixie," she cried, "I knew it would happen. You were bitten by a copperhead!"

"No, no," Trixie moaned, rocking to and fro. *"I'm* all right. It's the dogs. Honey, it's so horrible, I can't talk about it."

"The dogs?" Honey repeated. "Did they fall into a nest of copperheads? Trixie! Please answer me.

Are Reddy and Patch badly hurt? Are they—dead?"

Trixie raised her head. "Worse than that," she said sadly, "because if anybody finds out what they did, they'll be shot."

"Shot?" Honey's lovely face was very pale. "But why? What have they done?"

Trixie swallowed hard. "They killed a deer, Honey. I caught them sniffing around the carcass, and there was blood all over the place."

"I'm going to faint," Honey said and put her head down between her knees.

"Don't you dare faint," Trixie cried fiercely, although she felt like fainting herself. "We've got to pull ourselves together and do something about that carcass. If the boys should come across that dead deer, they'd guess right away who killed it. And then— Well, even though they love Patch and Reddy as much as we do, well, you know how ethical and honorable Jim and Brian are. Even Mart, especially now, when they've been hired to be game wardens."

Honey sat up. "But we're supposed to be game wardens, too, Trixie," she wailed. "So we've got to report what the dogs did."

"No, we don't," Trixie replied firmly. "We didn't see Reddy and Patch with our own eyes kill that deer. And chances are good that they'll never do such a thing again. Neither one of them alone would have or could have done it. It only happened because they were traveling in a team. It probably all started out as a game. They must have been running that deer since early this morning, and then, when he dropped from utter exhaustion, they—well, we don't know for sure, Honey. So if we bury the carcass and never let both dogs out together again at the same time, it'll never happen again."

"Oh, oh, I'm so confused," Honey moaned. "I hate the dogs for doing what they did, but I don't really hate them, because I don't think they meant to kill that lovely creature. But, Trixie, now that they have, they'll do it again and again. That's what always happens. Jim and Daddy were talking about it just last week. Pretty soon other dogs will join Patch and Reddy; then there'll be a pack. They'll kill one deer after another, and in the end they'll all have to be put away."

Trixie sniffed, but it sounded more like a sob. "I don't believe it," she said staunchly. "That's the way sheep-killing dogs behave, because they eat what they kill. Oh, woe," she yelled suddenly. "Why didn't I think of that before? Why didn't I call the dogs away from the carcass right away? Maybe they *are* eating it now."

Both girls began to call and whistle, and in a moment the dogs came bounding into the clearing. They were wagging their tails and very obviously expected to be welcomed with open arms.

"How can the two of them act so innocent?" Honey asked, looking at them sadly.

"They are innocent," Trixie said loudly. "And don't you forget it for one minute. Until somebody proves that they are guilty, I'm going to go right on believing there is a poacher lurking around here. And it was that poacher who killed the deer." She swung up on Susie's back. "Please hand me the newspapers, Honey. We've got to take the dogs home right away and then come back here and bury the carcass."

Honey said nothing until they had cantered along the trail for several minutes with the dogs scampering beside the horses. Then she said soberly, "If a poacher killed that deer, why didn't we hear the shot?"

"Because he used a longbow, of course," Trixie said impatiently.

"Then why didn't you see the arrow in the—the carcass?" Honey asked.

"Oh, I don't know," Trixie cried. "I just took one look at the horrible scene and fled. Anyway, a deer can run for miles after it's been shot with a bow. The shaft of the arrow might have been broken off."

"I thought people always hunted deer very early in the morning," Honey went on.

"They usually do," Trixie agreed, "but the poacher might not have seen one until an hour ago. It would take him quite a while to follow and track it down to where it dropped."

"Then," Honey said in a more hopeful tone of voice, "if your theory is right, the carcass will be gone when we get back."

"That's right," Trixie said. "But to be on the safe side, we'll bring along spades."

Honey shook her head. "If we discover proof that the dogs did kill that deer, we'll have to tell Jim, Trixie. With Daddy away, he's the head of the family. And you know as well as I do, Trix, that he'll only laugh at us if we tell him we're going to keep the dogs shut up. That just couldn't be done. With all of the people who go in and out of our houses all day long, why, it's just about impossible. . . ." Her voice dwindled away.

"Oh, I know," Trixie said in a small voice. "Besides, we can't collect the money for being gamekeepers if we don't report the dogs. And if we don't get the money, Brian won't get his jalopy. Why does life always have to be so complicated?" she finished miserably.

"I know just how you feel," Honey said sympathetically. "I guess I don't love Patch quite as much as you love Reddy. We haven't had Patch anywhere near as long, and, anyway, he's Jim's dog. But don't forget that Jim's going to be just as brokenhearted as you are, Trixie. If he has to get rid of Patch, it'll just about kill him."

"Don't you think I know that?" Trixie demanded crossly. "That's one reason why I don't even want Jim to know. And have you forgotten about Bobby? You know how he absolutely adores the ground Reddy walks on! How do you suppose my baby brother is going to feel when we have to tell him that he's never going to see his dog again?"

At that, both girls reined in their horses and burst into tears. The dogs stopped, too, and sat on their haunches, tongues lolling. They were so young and alive and carefree and happy now, Trixie thought, but in a few more hours. . . .

"We just can't do it," she suddenly sobbed. "There are too many other people involved. Brian, for one. He'd much rather go without a jalopy than have anything happen to Reddy. Why, even Mart would let his hair grow if he thought it would make Reddy happy." Trixie tried to smile at her own joke but couldn't do much more than grimace. "Moms and Dad love Reddy just as much as though he were a member of our family, which he is."

Honey shook her head up and down. "Ditto for Patch at our house. We won't say anything to anybody about that deer, Trixie. We'll just resign as gamekeepers and spend all our time making sure the dogs don't do it again. If we don't let them form the habit of chasing deer, they'll probably never be tempted again."

Trixie brightened. "All right, but let's don't do anything until we go back to the clearing and make sure the carcass is still there. I'll gallop on ahead and give Dad the papers. I'll ask him to keep Reddy home while we finish patrolling the preserve. Dad'll understand. He knows what an awful pest Reddy is. Dad's great. He won't even ask any questions if I ride off with a spade. He'll just take if for granted that we're going to play polo with spades and use a porcupine instead of a ball. The way Alice in Wonderland did it, you know."

Honey was now laughing as hard as she had been crying before. "Alice used a flamingo instead of a spade, and she was playing croquet, but I see what you mean. Oh," she suddenly interrupted herself, "porcupines and hedgehogs and mice and rats and even ants. Do you follow me, Trix?"

Trixie gasped. "Yes! If we *don't* hurry back to that clearing and *do* let nature take its course, there won't be anything left of that carcass. I remember reading somewhere that ants dote on antlers and armies of them have been know to carry away the whole thing—branches, stem, and all—in no time flat."

Honey chortled ecstatically. "I know it isn't very honorable and ethical for us not to go right back to that clearing, Trix, before your army ant friends have a chance. But, after all, we can't do *every*-thing, and we've simply got to patrol the part of the preserve that spreads around on this side of Glen Road. After that it'll be time for lunch, and you've got to get glamorous for Ben after that, because he's arriving around two-thirty. So I just don't see how we can spend any more time patrolling the other side of the road, do you?"

"No," Trixie said emphatically. "Especially since that Thing we were talking about may well be, as Mart would say, nonexistent. If we should consult him, he probably would say that it was a figment of my imagination. As a matter of fact, I'm beginning to think that Mart is right. I dreamed up that whole ghastly scene." She tucked the roll of newspapers under her left arm and reached across the saddle to shake hands with Honey. "It was simply a daymare, as Bobby would say. Don't you agree that's what it must have been, Miss Wheeler?"

Honey bowed. "I do, Miss Belden. Meet you on the trail behind the stable in ten minutes." She trotted off along the shoulder of Glen Road with Patch leading the way. Reddy raced off toward Trixie's home, and, after a bit of encouragement, Trixie persuaded Susie to follow him. The glossy black mare obviously felt that she and the chestnut gelding, Starlight, were a team that should not be separated so abruptly. But, to Trixie's satisfaction, Reddy did not feel at all the same way about Patch.

"They're not a team yet," she muttered softly. "And as Regan would say, *single-handedly*, they'll probably never run down another deer, let alone kill one."

For deep down in her heart, Trixie did not really think that a poacher had killed that deer. She was sure that the dogs had done it. And if they ever even tried to do such a terrible thing again, she knew that the verdict would be a death sentence!

Guilty Consciences • 11

TRIXIE'S FATHER came out on the terrace in answer to her call and deftly caught the bundle of papers she tossed to him.

"You're a regular pony express," he said and produced a lump of sugar from the pocket of his jacket for Susie. "I'm sorry I asked you to get the papers, Trixie. I forgot about your job."

"It's all right, Dad." She smiled down at him. "We have to go right by Mr. Lytell's store when we patrol. It was no trouble at all."

"But stopping off and coming back here must have delayed you," he said, "and I know you're in a hurry to get through early today. Ben arrives this afternoon sometime, doesn't he, Trixie?"

Trixie felt her cheeks burn. She wanted to say, "Yes, and I couldn't care less, that crum-bum!" But instead she forced herself to mumble, "Uh-huh. We're all invited to dinner at the Manor House."

"That's nice," her father said. "But you mustn't stay up late. Don't forget you have to get up at dawn to patrol before school tomorrow." He frowned. "I don't want you to get overtired, and you mustn't let this job interfere with your homework."

Trixie laughed. "We haven't any homework, Dad, and we won't have any all week, on account of the Thanksgiving holidays beginning on Wednesday. All we're doing now in school is reviewing."

He reached up suddenly and touched her hand. "You look worried, Trix. Anything wrong?"

Trixie was sorely tempted to blurt out, "Yes, Dad, everything's wrong." But she somehow managed to swallow the lump in her throat and wordlessly shook her head. "I am sort of tired," she finally got out. "It isn't the patrolling. It's grooming the horses and cleaning the tack. You know how strict Regan is. Everything's got to be just perfect or he has a fit."

Mr. Belden chuckled. "Every rose has a thorn, and don't forget that Regan is one of your best friends." He gave her hand a good-bye pat and went up the steps to the terrace.

Trixie waved to him and trotted off down the

driveway. *I wish I dared tell Dad about the dogs and the deer*, she thought dismally. *I wish I could tell him that I despise Ben Riker. I wish—oh*, she suddenly interrupted herself, *I forgot to ask Dad to shut Reddy inside the house.*

But it was too late now, for the harum-scarum Irish setter had disappeared.

I hope Reddy's on the trail of a rabbit, as usual, she thought unhappily.

When they turned into the Wheelers' driveway, Susie, without any urging at all, began to gallop, and when she reached the stable, she stopped so short that Trixie almost fell off. Susie had obviously made up her mind that she had already had all of the exercise she needed that day. Until Trixie kicked her smartly with both heels, she refused to budge, and even then she stayed in one spot, bucking and rearing.

Regan came out of the tack room and handed Trixie a quirt. "Give her a good switching," he ordered. "She's got a stubborn streak." He grinned. "Like some kids around here whose names I won't mention."

Trixie knew better than to disobey Regan, but she hated to whip any horse and especially Susie, who was usually so docile. One smart tap on her hindquarters did the trick, however, and in another minute Trixie had joined Honey on the path that led into the northern part of the game preserve.

"I thought you'd never come," Honey complained as they trotted along between the evergreens. "I'm suffering from an awful guilty conscience already. Patch came all the way home with me, but he turned and ran right off again."

"So did Reddy," Trixie said. "But we can't do anything about that now, Honey. We've got to go out and patrol."

"I saw Mart," Honey said after a long silence. "He's working on the clubhouse roof. He says it takes only two people to repair the few feeding stations that were damaged. Brian and Jim are much better at that sort of thing."

"Where are *they?*" Trixie asked nervously. "I don't particularly want to see them, but I hope they're working on the other side of the road."

"They're not," Honey said dismally. "According to what Mart said, I gather they're working very close to that Thing you found."

Trixie forced herself to laugh, although she didn't feel a bit cheerful. "Knowing your sense of direction, my guess is that Brian and Jim are working several acres away from the Thing."

Honey didn't even smile. After another long silence, she said, "What are we going to do with Ben when he arrives? Mother'll have a fit if we ignore him, but we can't let him patrol with us. If we did, he'd demand part of the pay."

"And we certainly don't want him fooling around the clubhouse," Trixie said. "His idea of a good joke would be to set it on fire or something."

"That's the point," Honey said worriedly. "But if we don't keep an eye on him, he might do something dreadful like playing a practical joke on Regan. He might fill the saddle-soap cans with cold cream or tie knots in the reins."

Trixie shuddered. "What a goon! And I have to be nice to him."

Honey smiled suddenly as she went on to add, "More than that, you have to act as though you were in love with him."

"Rub it in; rub it in," Trixie said sarcastically. "I'll have you know, Honey Wheeler, I don't have to put on that act unless there's an audience. That means that when I'm alone with him, which I hope will never happen, or when you and I are alone with him, I can pretend he isn't there. So let's do all we can to keep me away from him when the others are around. Thus, the answer to the whole ghastly Ben Riker problem is to make the boys keep an eye on him. We'll just tell them flatly that they have to. After all, he *is* a boy."

Honey giggled. "They'll flatly refuse to cope with him unless he's in a straitjacket, and you know it. But seriously, Trix, he isn't awful *all* of the time. He can be very nice and lots of fun when he isn't playing practical jokes."

"You're wasting your breath on me," Trixie said sourly. "Sell Ben's good points to Jim. Make *him* love him as though he were a beloved sibling, and all of our problems will be solved."

"Don't be silly," Honey interrupted. "Jim despises boys like Ben who have too much spending money and never do any work. What—who—I mean, whom I was thinking of is Di Lynch. Ben is very good-looking in that playboy way, and Di is so pretty. If we introduced them, they might go for each other; then that would be that. All you'd have to do is look jealous for a while and then brokenhearted, and pretty soon you could become resigned to your fate and be your normal self again."

Trixie burst into loud, joyous laughter. "You're a genius, Honey. Di is the perfect answer. Invite her out this afternoon."

Honey nodded. "If they get along today, I'll ask her to spend the whole Thanksgiving vacation with us. Lucky for us, Miss Trask likes house parties. She'll be sure to approve."

"Only one thing worries me," Trixie said after a while. "Di might come out in jeans. That would ruin everything. Ben hates tomboys. How can we tactfully tell her to wear a dress?"

"I'll say we're having a little party," Honey said

calmly. "It's getting warmer by the minute, so we can have hot chocolate and cookies on the veranda around four o'clock, and with all of us there it *will* be a party, in a way."

"Well, count me out," Trixie said firmly. "I couldn't possibly stand a party today and again on Thursday, so soon after the wedding."

"What party is there going to be on Thursday?" Honey asked.

"Honey Wheeler!" Trixie cried. "You know Moms always asks a lot of people to drop in on Thanksgiving all afternoon and evening. Your parents and you and Jim were invited weeks ago. Miss Trask and Regan, too. It's what you call an open house, but it's a party just the same. Moms serves a buffet supper of ham and turkey and coleslaw and all, which I have to help her with and at the same time keep Bobby from doing any of the awful things he always does when we have company."

Trixie stopped for breath, and Honey said, "I knew you were having open house on Thursday, but I didn't think of it as a party, but of course it is. Your mother asked Ben, too. I hope she asked Di."

"All of the Lynches are coming," Trixie told her. "And the neighbors, of course. Dozens of people, but they seldom stay very long and don't all arrive at once. But let's get back to your party. Please, Honey, don't make me come to it."

"All right, I won't," Honey said, smiling. "But the boys are going to think it's awfully odd, after the way you've been saying all week that you could hardly wait until Ben arrives."

"Oh, I'll be here when he arrives, all right," Trixie said bitterly. "But I don't have to become his Siamese twin, do I? And there's no sense in your telling me I have to look jealous and brokenhearted and resigned. I don't know how to look any of those things."

"I'd love to see you try," Honey said wistfully. "It would be so funny." She glanced at her wristwatch. "Well, we've finished patrolling this section, and although we didn't do a very good job on the other side, there isn't time now. What with grooming the horses and cleaning the tack, we're going to be late to lunch."

It was almost one when they separated in front of the stable. Trixie raced home and scrubbed her hands at the kitchen sink. The other Beldens were already seated at the table, but nobody scolded her for being late.

"We've finished our share of the work," Brian told her. "How did the patrolling go?"

"Fine," Trixie said. "Just fine."

"How many poachers did you two catch?" Mart asked derisively as she pulled out her chair. "And where did you leave their corpses?"

Trixie jumped guiltily and hastily changed the subject. "What about grain for the birds? When do we scatter that around?"

"Jim and I took care of that today," Brian said. "I'm not sure when it has to be done again, but Jim will let you know." He turned to his father. "Jim sure is great, Dad. He seems to know everything about everything."

They began to discuss the work they were doing on the clubhouse then, and Trixie ate in silence. There was so much to be done and so little time to do it all in. After lunch she washed the dishes and hurried up to take a shower. It was agony to have to waste time getting dressed up for Ben's arrival, because just as soon as she could, she was going to go home and change back into jeans. Then she would bike along the road to the trail that led into the game preserve. After that she would have to walk until she reached the clearing where the Thing was. *If* the Thing was still there! She shuddered just thinking about it.

For, slowly but surely, Trixie had come to the conclusion that she could not sleep that night until she made sure, one way or the other, about the dogs. If they were the culprits, she knew that she would have to tell Jim. But if they weren't, then the terrible weight on her conscience would disappear.

A Baffling Discovery • 12

TRIXIE WORE a pleated dark-blue wool skirt and a pullover dark-blue cashmere sweater that matched. She even polished her school loafers so they didn't look quite so scuffed, and clasped around her neck a strand of small pearls that Di had donated to the cause.

Then all of a sudden it dawned on her that today of all days she should be wearing her ring. In fact, she should wear it every time she got dressed up all week. After all the fuss she had made, somebody, if not everybody in the family, would be sure to notice that she never wore it.

"Oh, woe," Trixie moaned as she started up the

hill to the Manor House, "why do I get myself into these scrapes? I wish Jim had never given me that ring."

What could she do to solve this problem?

"Nothing," she decided and trudged along until she caught sight of the boys and girls who were waiting for her on the veranda. By the time she arrived, Jim, Brian, and Mart were leaving to continue work on the clubhouse.

They glanced at her with pity, shrugged and sighed as one man, and departed. This suited Trixie fine, because now she didn't have to put on her act. Then she noticed to her satisfaction that Di, looking prettier than ever, had already captivated Ben.

He stared at Trixie for a moment as though he didn't know who she was, then said coolly, "Hi, goon. Go home and take off your mother's clothes. On you they definitely look queer."

Honey said quickly, "You look darling, Trixie. Come on up to my room with me for a sec. I want to show you something." She winked at Di. "It's about the secret. *You* know."

Di winked back with an understanding smile and said to Ben, "Let's play some of our favorite records. I'm so glad you like country songs, too."

"Wow!" Trixie exploded when she and Honey were alone upstairs. "Di's got him, hook, line, and sinker. How in the world *can* she stand him?"

"Oh, Trixie," Honey cried. "He's really very good-looking. Tall and broad-shouldered and blond and all. But let's not talk about him. What worries me is your ring. You've simply got to wear it every now and then. If you don't, your father will think you lost it."

"I wish I had," Trixie said mournfully. "I mean, I wish I were a liar so I could tell him I'd lost it when he asks me where it is. Which he's going to do pretty soon."

Honey nodded. "If you keep your hands in your pockets, you might get by with it for a while. But you can't do that at your Thanksgiving party."

"I can't do it and eat dinner every evening, either," Trixie pointed out tartly. Suddenly she brightened. "Now that Di has broken my heart and all, do I have to dress up for dinner every night?"

Honey thought for a moment. "I guess not, but you've simply got to look sad for at least a couple of days."

"I *am* sad," Trixie retorted. "I'm so darn sad, I'm thinking seriously of running away from home and staying until I can get that ring back from Mr. Lytell."

Honey laughed. "Now you're talking like Bobby. Every time he gets into a scrape, he runs away. Thank goodness he never runs any farther than your chicken coop or Regan's apartment over the garage."

Trixie shrugged. "Most of the time Bobby doesn't have sense enough to know when he's done something awful. Remember what a scare he gave us when he lost that diamond we found in the clubhouse, when it was still the gatehouse?"

"He didn't lose it," Honey reminded her. "He put it accidentally in the safest possible place."

"Oh!" Trixie slid off the window seat and raced over to Honey's dainty dressing table. She grabbed the jewel box and brought it back to Honey. "This thing is jam-packed with costume jewelry. There must be a phony diamond ring in it that looks enough like mine so I can wear it for a week."

Honey gasped. "Trixie, you're so smart. There *is* one somewhere." She dumped the contents on the window seat, and they both stared at the jumbled mass of pins, necklaces, earrings, bracelets, and rings. "I don't know where one thing begins and another one ends," Honey complained as she tried to disentangle the various bright stones and strands.

Trixie held her breath until they were all sorted; then she let it out in a long, discouraged sigh. "Nine rings, but not one of them with anything that faintly resembles a diamond. And you're supposed to be my best friend, Honey Wheeler."

Honey giggled. "Have no fears, I shall not fail you. I remember now where that diamond ring is. Mother borrowed it from me when she went to a masquerade as the Queen of Sheba. It must be in her costume jewelry box." She led the way down the hall and into Mrs. Wheeler's beautiful room. She marched over to the dressing table, lifted the cover on a handsome leather case, took out a tray, and cried triumphantly, "Behold, comrade! In fact, take your choice. There are four, to be exact."

Trixie peered over Honey's shoulder. "Are you sure these are all fakes?" she asked in an awed tone.

"Of course," Honey replied. "They're not even good paste imitations. Mother has tons of those, of course, which look exactly like her valuable jewels, but they're so expensive to make, she keeps them under lock and key. All the stuff in this box is just junk she wears for fun." She took out one of the rings. "This looks enough like yours so if you don't get too close to somebody who knows all about precious stones, you'll get by with it."

Trixie hesitated before she slipped it on her finger. "It's kind of loose," she murmured nervously. "Suppose I lose it? How much is it worth, Honey?"

"About a dollar," Honey said airily. "Anyway, it's mine, so don't worry. I hereby give it to you, to have and to hold or to lose, but please don't lose it until you get your own back."

"Gee, thanks," Trixie said as they went back into Honey's room. For a moment she felt guilty. Honey was such a good friend! She really should tell her that she was going to go back and examine the Thing. But if she did, Honey would argue against it. She would be very sympathetic, but she would say, "I know just how you feel. I won't be able to sleep tonight, either, because of my guilty conscience. But it'll be dark before you get there. You might get lost in the labyrinth. The dogs will be shut up indoors all night, so tomorrow morning, when we patrol before school, will be soon enough."

Right now Honey was saying, "I wish you'd stay for hot chocolate and cookies, Trix. The boys are coming to my little party, because it'll be too dark to work on the clubhouse after four-thirty. We won't have much fun without you, but I know just how you feel. You'd have to put on an act and pretend to be jealous, and you must be awfully tired, what with the chores you have to do at home and all." She linked her arm through Trixie's, and they strolled down the stairs. "Jim and I think you're just wonderful, Trixie. Practically perfect. So don't pay any attention to Ben when he makes stupid remarks. I mean, don't stay away from here all week on account of him. The house party is all set. Di has accepted. I invited her for the whole vacation when I asked her to come out today, because I suddenly remembered that she and Ben are both music-lovers. They'll probably spend the whole time listening to records, so we won't ever see them, except at meals." She stopped to catch her breath.

Trixie hugged her arm. "You're the one who's wonderful, Honey," she said softly. "Practically perfect. Don't worry about the house party. It's going to be great. But I've got to go now. It must be four o'clock." She broke away from Honey and ran off.

Back at home, Trixie hastily changed into blue jeans and high wool socks. As she slipped her cashmere sweater over her head, the prongs in the setting of Honey's ring got caught in the sleeve, and the ring came off, too. Impatiently Trixie plucked it free and tossed it into her top bureau drawer. Then she donned her old heavy wool sweater and hurried downstairs. One good break was that her parents and Bobby had gone off for a drive after lunch. Without even telling a little white lie, Trixie had let them take it for granted that she was going to spend the whole afternoon and evening up at the Manor House.

At the garage, she hopped on her bike and coasted down the driveway. Then she pedaled along the road as fast as she could. The sun was a red ball cut in half by the tops of the towering evergreens in the distance. When the ball of fire dipped down completely into the Hudson River, it would grow dark very quickly. Too late, Trixie realized that she should have brought along a flashlight.

It was already gloomy in the woods when she turned off the trail and hid her bike in the bushes. Traveling on foot along that rocky path was very different from riding horseback on it. She soon found out that she couldn't walk fast without the risk of turning her ankle, and every time she came around a bend, the stretch that lay ahead of her seemed to be blacked out by shadows until her eyes grew accustomed to the dusk. Then, a few yards later, the waning light of the sun was almost blinding.

"I know how moles feel now," Trixie said to herself as she stumbled along. "No wonder they can't see when they come up from their underground tunnels every now and then."

In order to keep up her courage, she began to talk out loud: "I wish I were a mole or a bat or an owl. Do any of them eat carcasses? All that business about ants eating antlers was silly. There are only army ants in the tropics. They *can* demolish a carcass in a matter of hours, but there aren't any around here. . . . Mice eat antlers, though. I read about it in one of Brian's books. I hope there's an army of field mice in these woods. . . . Foxes and catamounts are scavengers, too, but not as thorough as buzzards and jackals. . . . Coyotes do a good job, but they don't eat antlers. All of the million buffalo horns that have been whitening for ages on the deserts out west are proof of that. Besides, none of the coyotes, which are called brush wolves in the Adirondacks, would come all the way down here just to eat up a dead deer. But there are plenty of big wildcats. That's why that little purple mountain over there is called Catamount Hill. I wish it were closer. . . . No, I don't. Catamounts are supposed to be cowards, but that all depends on your definition of coward. I'm scared to death right now, and I think I'm lost, but you don't see me running away, do you? *Not that I'd know in which direction to run. . . .*"

For Trixie was lost now. So long as she could see an inch of the sunset between the evergreens, she knew where west was, but now there was only a pale green light in the sky—a yellowish green, which usually meant that a storm of some sort was on the way. The air was growing colder, too, and there was a moistness in it, which, Trixie felt sure, meant that it would snow before morning.

She stumbled along, her teeth chattering as much from cold as from nervousness, and all of a sudden found herself at the fork where Honey had waited for her with the horses that morning. Now she knew exactly where she was and, in a matter of minutes, burst into the other small clearing. There were no shadows here, and neither was there any sign whatsoever that a dead deer had ever lain in that spot.

Trixie rubbed her eyes. "I must have been dreaming, after all." She knelt, straining her eyes, and then she saw the impression the body of the deer had made in the bed of pine needles. And some of the red brown leaves were that color because blood had been splattered on them. There were also unmistakable signs that a human had eviscerated the carcass at this very spot. Trixie knew about these internal organs of animals because she had often cleaned chickens after her brothers had killed and plucked them. Her mother had carefully taught her how to "draw" a bird, so now Trixie was what the family called an "expert butcher." The heart, liver, and gizzard were used for gravy-making. The lungs and such, or "lights" as professional butchers called them, were broiled into a rich broth for mixing with dehydrated dog food—for Reddy.

Trixie sank to her knees. Reddy and Patch weren't the culprits after all, thank goodness. All over the damp soil in the clearing were tiny pawprints that proved that other, smaller animals had done the scavenging job after the human took the venison away. Bluejays had probably swooped down, too, for their share. Jim would know, even in the gloom, exactly what animals and birds had been there. It was Jim who had taught Trixie how to tell the difference between the footprint of a fox and the footprint of a dog. There was an enormous difference in the pawprint of members of the cat family, and Trixie was glad to see that no cat had been near the spot. Not yet, anyway. It wasn't dark enough for the catamounts to prowl.

Then all of a sudden she saw tracks that made her eyes feel as though they were popping out of her head. Bike-tire tracks! Not double, but single-tire tread marks. She followed them across the clearing to the spot where they disappeared on the pine-needle carpet of a narrow path. It wasn't possible, but it was true. Nobody, not even a circus performer, could have ridden any kind of a bike along the muddy paths and trails of these woods. But the tire tread marks proved that somebody had!

A Peculiar Poacher • 13

TRIXIE GROPED her way along the narrow path for a few yards, then returned to the spot where the single bike-tire tread disappeared. Visions of tight-rope walkers and performing seals danced dizzily through her head as she started back to the fork. Only one thought was comforting: The dogs were not the culprits. They might, tempted by the sport of it, have chased a wounded deer, but they had certainly not killed and eviscerated it. A human had done that, and that human must be a poacher.

It was almost pitch-dark when Trixie reached the small clearing near the fork, and because of the shadows, she hardly knew which way to turn. By groping blindly, she finally discovered the difference between the narrow paths and the wider trail, and stumbled along it. It seemed to wind through the branches of evergreens interminably. Just when she was sure she had reached the spot where she had hidden her bike, she found that she had emerged from the game preserve onto Glen Road at the very spot where the path, not the trail, ended opposite Mr. Lytell's store.

"Now when could I have left the trail?" Trixie asked herself as she trudged along the road. She was sure of only one thing: Nothing would induce her to go back into those shadowy woods except in broad daylight. The road was dark enough as it was, but she knew it so well that it wasn't long before she was back on her bike, pedaling the rest of the way home.

When she got there, her parents and Bobby were having supper, and they stared at her in amazement. "Why, Trixie," Mrs. Belden cried, "we thought you were at the Wheelers'. Didn't Ben Riker arrive, after all?"

"Oh, yes," Trixie told her. "But so did Di Lynch. They're crazy about each other." She tried her best to look jealous and heartbroken and resigned but had a feeling that she only looked rather silly. She could see that both her father and mother were trying hard not to smile.

"Well," said Mrs. Belden, "have supper with us, then. Macaroni with cheese-and-tomato sauce and salad. Bring me a plate, Trixie, and I'll serve you."

Trixie was starving, so she had two helpings of everything. Her father chuckled and quoted: " 'Men have died and worms have eaten them, but not for love.' You're living proof of that Shakespearean bit of wisdom, Trixie." He leaned across the table. "Tell me. Wasn't Ben impressed when you flashed your ring in his face? Or did you make the mistake of greeting him dressed as you are?"

"Oh, I got all dressed up," Trixie said hastily. "But Di is so pretty, I knew right away that it wasn't any use."

"M-m-m," her father said thoughtfully. "Well, if you've decided to be normal again, I imagine you'll want me to put your ring back in the vault. It's hardly the appropriate accessory for the costume you're now wearing."

"Oh, Dad," Trixie cried. "You said I could keep the ring a week. You promised."

"So I did," he agreed. "But, with the possible exception of our Thanksgiving party, I can't imagine when you'll want it."

"Every evening," Trixie said, hating the thought of it, "I'm going to get dressed up. I mean, the Wheelers are having a house party because Di's spending the holidays there, too. Miss Trask is sure to ask Brian and Mart and me to a lot of meals. Their dinners are always formal. I can't go there looking like this."

"Of course you can't," Mrs. Belden put in. "Your father's only teasing, Trixie. But I don't understand why you're not up at the Wheelers' now. What happened? Why did you come back here and change your clothes?" She took a stack of dishes out to the kitchen, beckoning for Trixie to follow. When they had cleared the maple dining table, she said, "I'll wash and you can dry, honey. I don't mean to pry into your affairs, and if you don't want to answer my questions, don't. It's just that you look so worried, and I can't believe that it's because of Di and Ben."

Trixie gulped. Her mother and father were such good sports. But they wouldn't approve of the whole business about the ring. And it would be awfully hard to explain why she hadn't told Jim about the dead deer. Parents could be understanding some times, but so often they couldn't understand why you did things that seemed wrong but that were perfectly right.

Suddenly Trixie realized that Jim, in a way, was like her parents. Although she knew now that the dogs weren't the culprits, she couldn't tell him about the deer. He would be furious because she hadn't told him right away, while there was still time for him and Brian to have caught the poacher. Mart, when and *if* he ever heard about it, wouldn't be furious, but he would tease her unmercifully and would call her a "lame-brain" from morning to night.

No, the boys must never know, so there was only one answer to the problem: She and Honey must track down and catch the poacher . . . *all by themselves!*

Aloud she said quite truthfully to her mother, "I am worried, Moms. It's about the gamekeeper job. It's more of a responsibility than I thought it would be."

Mrs. Belden nodded sympathetically. "You and Honey have an awful lot of territory to cover. So, since you have to get up so early tomorrow morning, I think you ought to go to bed right away."

Trixie, feeling more guilty than ever, shook her head. "I'll put Bobby to bed first, Moms," she offered. "He'll go up right away if I promise to read the funny papers to him."

"That would be just wonderful," Mrs. Belden said gratefully. "He was a dickens all during the drive we took this afternoon. He promised to rest quietly in the backseat, because I didn't make him take a nap, but instead he jumped up and down constantly and asked a steady stream of questions."

"Oh, Moms," Trixie cried. "I should have stayed home with Bobby while you and Dad went for a drive alone. You must be awfully tired."

"Not physically tired," her mother said cheerfully. "But I am rather tired of Bobby. A little of his conversation goes a long way." She gave Trixie a hug. "He's sure to be tired, too, so I don't think you'll have to read to him for very long. Make sure that he brushes his teeth properly. He's recently acquired the habit of wetting the toothbrush and licking the powder off the palm of his hand, and then he informs me that his teeth are clean."

They laughed together, and Trixie hurried into the living room, where Bobby was trying to persuade his father to read the comics to him.

"I'll do it, Bobby." Trixie took his fat little hand. "Come on. As soon as you've brushed your teeth and climbed into bed, I'll read *Peter Rabbit.*"

He pulled his hand away and then stared at her hand. "Hey! You're not wearing your ring. Betcha you losted it."

"Don't be silly," Trixie said quickly. "Ladies don't wear rings when they're wearing blue jeans."

"Hey," he jeered. "You're not a lady."

Trixie hastily gathered the funny papers and handed them to him. "You carry these while I go ahead and turn down the covers on your bed."

He followed her upstairs without another word and, after both threats and bribes, brushed his teeth thoroughly. But Trixie had hardly tucked him into bed when he began to ask questions again about her ring. She knew that he was peevish because he was so tired, and she tried to be patient.

"Betcha you losted it," he insisted. "Betcha you losted it. Hey! Betcha you losted it."

Trixie was finally forced to go into her room and scrabble through her top bureau drawer until she found the imitation that Honey had loaned her. She gave it to Bobby and asked exasperatedly, "Now are you satisfied that I haven't lost it? You and your one-track mind!"

The phrase, one-track, immediately reminded her of the single-tire tread tracks she had discovered in the clearing. She shivered involuntarily, remembering how awful it had been to be lost in those dark woods. She might still be there, and by now the catamounts would be prowling.

Bobby brought her back to the present by yelling, "Take your old ring. I don't want it. Read *Peter Rabbit.*" Fretfully he tossed the ring at her. "Read, *read*, READ!"

Trixie picked it up and slipped it on her finger. "You shouldn't throw things, Bobby. How would you like it if I started throwing some of your valuable things at you?"

Instantly he was all smiles. "Throw my panda at me. Let's play catch. Throw my panda at me."

Trixie couldn't help laughing. "It's too late for games. Now, move over so I can sit beside you.

We'll read the funnies together. Your teacher at school says you read very well, Bobby." She pointed to the paper. "I'm sure you know this word. T-h-e. What is it?"

"Ted," he said promptly. "It's short for teddy bear. I want my teddy bear—*and* my panda. Read, *read*, READ!"

He nestled down on the pillow, cuddling the two battered stuffed animals, and in less than five minutes was sound asleep. Trixie tiptoed out of the room and into her own room across the hall. There she carefully put Honey's ring into the handkerchief box that her Aunt Alicia had given her as a birthday present.

"I've got to be more careful of that imitation," she scolded herself. "If I'd lost it, Bobby would have talked about it until everyone was suspicious." A few minutes later she toppled into bed and fell asleep almost immediately.

When Trixie awoke before dawn the next morning, she found that snow had fallen during the night. But, although the air was crisp and cold now, she knew that when the sun was high in the sky, the white carpet would have disappeared. Honey—holding both horses, which she had already saddled and bridled—was patiently waiting for her in front of the Wheeler stable.

"B-r-r," she said as they mounted. "It's fuh-reez-ing. I'm wearing fur-lined gloves, and here's a pair for you. Starlight and Strawberry are feeling their oats like anything. If our fingers grow numb, we'll never be able to hold them down."

The horses were so full of pep that they started right off at a canter. "Rarin' to go," Trixie agreed. "At this rate, we'll cover the whole north end of the preserve easily before breakfast." They fairly flew along the trails, so there was no sense in trying to talk until, at last, the horses were willing to slow down to a trot. Then Trixie told Honey about the strange single-tire track she had discovered the afternoon before.

"A unicycle," Honey gasped. "I didn't know there were any except in circuses."

"Is that what you call a one-wheeled bike?" Trix-ie asked.

Honey giggled. "Of course, as in *uni*corn. The *bi* in bicycle means that it has two wheels. I think it's Greek, like Phi Beta Kappa."

"It's all Greek to me," Trixie said with a grin. "Even if I do get better marks in math so I graduate from high school and go to college, nobody's ever going to give me a Phi Beta Kappa key."

"Oh, I don't know," Honey said cheerfully. "Jim is sure to get one. He'll give you his."

"That will be the day," Trixie retorted. "Jim

wouldn't even give me the time of day. All he'll do, if you tell him about that dead deer, is give me a good bawling out."

"I won't tell him a thing," Honey promised. "I'm so glad you got proof that the dogs didn't do it, Trixie, but you shouldn't have gone into those awful woods alone when it was dark. Now that we know there's a crazy person loose in there, promise me you'll never do it again."

"Crazy person?" Trixie pulled Strawberry down to a walk and then a stop. Starlight promptly stopped, too, and lowered his head to lick at the melting snow. "What do you mean by *crazy*, Honey?"

Honey shrugged her slim shoulders. "Nobody but a crazy person would try to ride a unicycle along those paths. Why, you can hardly ride a horse along them. Anyway, nobody but a circus performer would own a unicycle."

"That's true," Trixie admitted. "But circus people don't know how to butcher a deer. Whoever toted away that venison, antlers and all, was an expert butcher. An amateur would have chopped off the head and left it there. But experts know that deer drain better if they are hung up by their antlers. The meat has to be aged before you can eat it, and in cold weather like this, a deer can hang for a month without spoiling."

"You're much too smart for me," Honey said. "How do you know so much about venison?"

"From people like Tom Delanoy," Trixie replied. "He taught Brian and Mart how to shoot and fish, you know, and I used to tag along after them until Bobby got to the age where I had to stay home and keep *him* from tagging along."

Honey said nothing while they cantered back toward the stable. The sky in the east was now aquamarine and golden pink, as the rising sun scattered purples and blues. There were only little wisps of snow on the downward slopes, and by the time they reached the stable, there was no snow at all on the driveway.

Regan met them at the door. "I'll groom the horses and clean the tack," he said. "You kids have barely got time to dress and eat your breakfast before the school bus arrives."

"Oh, thanks," Honey breathed. "But you shouldn't really do it for us, Regan. It's all part of our job as gamekeepers."

"Not necessarily," he said. "All I ask is that you do a good job as gamekeepers and keep the horses exercised at the same time."

Later, when they met at the bus stop down by the road, Honey said to Trixie, "I still think he's crazy."

Trixie giggled. "If you're talking about Regan, I agree with you. The reason why he hated Fleagle was that Fleagle didn't groom his horse or clean the tack. Why he suddenly lets us get by—"

"Don't be silly," Honey hissed. "Of course I'm not talking about Regan. He's just being a good sport because he knows, as he said to Miss Trask last night, that we've bitten off more than we can chew. Don't worry about Regan's mentality. Soon as the holidays begin, he'll make us groom and clean and everything again. He's already got things fixed so Ben has to work, too, starting this very morning."

"Ben—work?" Trixie blinked. "Why, that creep faints from utter exhaustion if he has to change a phonograph needle."

"That's not true," Honey said, glancing worriedly over her shoulder at the boys who were strolling toward them. "Ben himself offered to work. He's got his driver's license now, you know, and he's going to do all of the chauffeuring while Tom's away. That, of course, made Miss Trask and Regan very happy."

Trixie nodded soberly. "It explains why Regan was so charming to us. I guess the answer is that Ben hasn't had his license long enough to consider driving as work. I just hope Miss Trask keeps him so busy he won't have time for any practical jokes." She lowered her voice. "Is Ben the person that you think is crazy? If so, I agree."

The boys were so close to them now that Honey

could only reply by whispering into Trixie's ear: "No, dopey. The *poacher!*"

Then suddenly Trixie realized that Honey was right. Nobody in his right mind would own a unicycle. And even if he did, he wouldn't ride one while out poaching. It didn't make sense. You just couldn't ride a unicycle and carry a slaughtered deer at the same time!

Mart Asks Questions • 14

THAT'S THE ANSWER, of course," Trixie said decisively. The girls had met at the stable after school and were now patrolling the southern part of the game preserve. "There must be two people loose in these woods—a poacher and a performer who has run away from a circus."

Honey laughed nervously. Although they hadn't wasted a minute since they got off the bus, the sun was already dipping down below the tree line, and it was gloomy in the thickly wooded sections of the preserve. "People don't escape from circuses," she told Trixie. "Circuses aren't insane asylums."

"Well," Trixie retorted, "insane asylums don't dish

out unicycles to the inmates, and only a lunatic would try to ride any kind of a cycle in these woods."

"Maybe it's easier with only one wheel," Honey said thoughtfully. "I mean, if you know how."

"Which *I* don't," Trixie replied. "And I still think that two wheels must be easier than one, just like two heads are better than one."

Honey shuddered. "Don't! You just gave me a mental picture of a two-headed monster riding around on a unicycle. I'd rather see a Cyclops riding on a unicorn."

Trixie shook with laughter, although she felt rather nervous, too. Tracking down a plain, ordinary poacher was one thing, but simultaneously tracking down a crazy unicyclist was quite another. The poacher had some reason for lurking around in the woods, but the unicyclist— Even if you told him he was trespassing, he probably wouldn't care. He'd probably utter an eerie chuckle and pedal off to the hollow tree he lived in. "I think he's more like a leprechaun than a Cyclops," Trixie said to Honey. "Or do I mean a dryad? Anyway, if he doesn't live in a hollow tree, where does he live?"

"For that matter," Honey replied, "where does the poacher live? If he's big enough to carry off a deer, he couldn't fit into a hollow tree. It snowed last night and was awfully cold, so he couldn't have slept right out in the open, could he?"

"That," Trixie said, "is what we've got to find out. He's probably pitched a tent somewhere."

Honey shuddered again. "That means leaving the trails to explore the paths. I positively won't. It's too scary early in the morning and late in the afternoon. Besides, even in broad daylight we'd be sure to get lost."

"School closes at noon on Wednesday—day after tomorrow," Trixie reminded her. "We can explore the paths then. We *have* to, Honey. We can't let that poacher keep shooting your father's deer. He's probably killing partridges and pheasants, too. Big New York City restaurants pay an awful lot of money for game. I think some of them even buy through a black market."

"Oh, Trixie," Honey begged, "don't let your imagination run away with you. That deer you saw yesterday was probably killed by a hunter who didn't know he was trespassing. Maybe he's gone away and won't come back. I mean, most men have jobs, so they can't go shooting except on weekends or holidays. Please, let's forget about him or else tell the boys."

"We can't do either," Trixie said firmly. "If Jim and Brian knew what we know, they'd spend all their time trying to catch that poacher. Then they'd never finish fixing the clubhouse. You heard what Brian said on the bus this morning. The snow last night didn't help matters any. We were lucky that it wasn't a blizzard."

"I know," Honey said. "At breakfast this morning, Jim told me that the snow had seeped down onto the curtains and furniture. They're not exactly ruined, but they'll never look quite as nice as they did."

"How about our equipment in the storeroom?" Trixie asked. "If the runners on our skates and sleds get too rusty, they *will* be ruined. And lots of the other stuff will get mildewed and rot away."

"That's what worries me most," Honey admitted. "I wish we dared move our equipment to the *Robin* until the roof is fixed. But we can't, not without permission from Tom and Celia, and they're somewhere in Canada."

"It's all hopeless," Trixie agreed. "If our sports equipment is ruined, we won't have any fun this winter, because we could never, never earn the money to buy more until we're practically as old as Methuselah."

"Maybe it won't snow again until the roof is fixed," Honey said. "Let's hope so." They cantered along in silence for a while; then she said, "I know it isn't very honorable and all, Trixie, but let's do forget about that poacher. I mean, if you had never left the trail, you would never have seen that dead deer. And the boys ordered us never to leave the trails. So, you see, it really amounts to the same thing as a bad dream. The only reason why I was upset yesterday was because I thought the dogs had done it and would do it again and again. What's one deer, anyway?"

"All right," Trixie said reluctantly. "It *was* a nightmare, especially the part about your friend, the two-headed unicyclist. I must have dreamed that up, hollow tree and all."

Honey sighed with relief. "Let's talk about something cheerful for a change. Di's going to bring a suitcase to school on Wednesday and ride home on the bus with us. She wants to help us patrol, but she doesn't really ride well enough, so I told her no, her job was to keep Ben from playing any practical jokes. She likes him a lot, so she didn't think that was much of a job. Is there anything we can ask Di to do so she'll feel she's being helpful?"

"Yes," Trixie promptly replied. "She and Ben both can keep an eye on Bobby while we patrol. Otherwise, a lot of the time while there's no school, I'll have to do it. It's part of my job, you know, and one thing I will say for Ben, he likes Bobby. He'd never play any practical jokes on *him*."

"That's true," Honey agreed. "Di adores Bobby. Everybody does, even though he is so mischievous. He can sort of chaperone Di and Ben while the rest of us work. I hope he likes country music."

"He does," Trixie said, "but not for long. You

know Bobby. He never stays in one place longer than a half hour unless he's asleep. But that's going to be Di's worry, not ours."

By that time it was dusk, and they had just barely covered all of the trails in the preserve. "I'm glad horses can see in the semidark," Honey said. "But we'd better keep them down to a walk from now on. They might stumble over a boulder, and, anyway, we've got to let them cool off or Regan will have a fit."

Trixie pulled Susie over to one side so Honey and Lady could lead the way. "I'm lost," she admitted. "I never saw any of these landmarks before. If you can call them landmarks."

"I can't, and I don't," Honey said with a giggle. "They're all just black blobs to me. I suppose people like Jim would call them trees and shadows. I'll give Lady her head. She'll take us home."

Lady did, and the girls were surprised to find that the boys were at the stable. Jim was putting a saddle on Jupiter, Brian was saddling Starlight, and Mart was leading Strawberry out of his stall.

"Are you boys crazy?" Honey demanded, swinging out of her saddle. "You can't go riding at this time of night. Anyway, all of the horses have been exercised. Regan himself gave Jupe a good workout this morning while Trixie and I were riding Starlight and Strawberry."

Jim glared at her. "Where have you two goons been? We were about to form a small posse and go search for your bodies."

"No, no," Mart corrected him. "You have forgotten, sheriff. We were perfectly willing to leave our sisters in the labyrinth forever. It was the horses we were about to seek. They are valuable, which is something I cannot say for the feminine members of our club."

As Trixie dismounted, Brian grabbed her arm. "You're up to something," he said. "Staying out so late, and disappearing so mysteriously yesterday. What cooks?"

Trixie jerked away from him. "It can't be very late. All we did was patrol the preserve on the other side of the road. If you think you can do it faster than we did, smarty, try it—just for size. I can't wait to hear what Regan's going to say to you when you bring a sweaty horse back to the stable, especially on a cold night like this."

"You can't win," Mart moaned. He put Strawberry back into the stall while the other boys followed suit and returned the saddles to the tack room. Then all three of them lounged against a wall of the stable while Trixie and Honey groomed Susie and Lady. "Not bad, but not good," Mart kept saying. "Like cheese, they'll improve with age; don't you agree, Jim?"

Jim nodded. "But I've been figuring it out mathematically, men. They had to cover a lot of ground between four and six-thirty, so I've come to the conclusion that, after all, they didn't get lost, nor did they loiter."

"Well, in that case," Brian said, "let's clean the tack for them."

Honey tossed her head. "Don't bother. Just, please, get out of our way."

"I wish they'd get off the face of the earth," Trixie said grimly. "Such morons should not be allowed in the same interplanetary system with us." She deliberately stepped on Mart's toe as she strode past him.

He punched her lightly on the arm. "Pardon me for living, but the graveyard's full." He followed her into the tack room. "Come on, sis, 'fess up. You're in some sort of a scrape, and you know it."

Honey came quickly to the rescue. "Oh, my goodness," she cried exasperatedly. "Can't you leave her alone? Don't you know that her heart is broken and all because Ben is so crazy about Di?"

"So *that's* it." Jim abruptly left the stable. Brian, with a puzzled expression on his handsome face, followed him out into the darkness.

Mart simply leaned against the edge of the worktable and began to whistle, saying after a while, "Don't you girls try to give *me* any of that. You almost had me fooled for a while, Trix. But when you disappeared so mysteriously yesterday afternoon, instead of lurking around and waving your diamond ring in Ben's face, I knew that you had simply been using him for an excuse." He lowered his voice to a whisper. *"Why did you ask Dad for the ring, and where is it now?"*

"None of your business," Trixie retorted.

"Did you pawn it?" Mart persisted. "Or lose it?"

It was Honey who replied. "Neither, Mart Belden, and it *is* none of your business. If you knew the real reason why Trixie asked her father for the ring, you'd die of shame."

"So?" His sandy eyebrows shot up. "The plot thickens. Mr. Lytell, among others, is very, very suspicious. He saw Trixie emerge from the woods yesterday after dark. He asked me to give him some explanation of why she was there at that time of the evening." Mart waved his hands. "I passed it off by explaining that you girls were gamekeepers and Trix must have been working overtime. He thought it odd, as I did, that she should patrol on foot at such a weird hour of the day."

"Oh, all right, Mart," Trixie suddenly exploded. "I'll tell you the truth, but you've got to promise not to tell Jim and Brian."

He raised his right hand. "Wild horses couldn't drag it out of me."

Trixie replaced the top on the saddle-soap can

and squeezed the sponge dry. Then she went over to the window to make sure that Brian and Jim had gone into the big house. "It's this way, Mart," she confided. "I found a dead deer in the preserve yesterday, so I know there's a poacher lurking around. I want to catch him, but Honey thinks that maybe he was just a hunter who trespassed by accident and probably won't ever come back."

Mart slid off the table and began to pace up and down in the tack room. "I'm inclined to agree with Honey," he said at last. "But the adventurous part of my personality agrees with you, Trix. To capture a poacher would be a feather in our caps. So let's not leave a stone or a leaf unturned."

Honey sighed. "Don't be silly, Mart. The important thing right now is to get the roof of the clubhouse fixed. That'll never be done if you're going to go galloping around looking for clues."

"True," he said, "but I have no intention of galloping or Sherlocking. I will simply provide Trixie with a few facts about snares and traps and such. Thus, if she doesn't fall into them, she will be able to recognize same. The point is this: A poacher worth catching is one who makes a business of it. That kind of a poacher rarely uses a gun. He shoots deer with a longbow, in or out of season. He sets snares for partridge and pheasant, in or out of season. Instead of using a rod and reel, he catches fish in a net. Those guys," he finished, "are a menace, and they ought to be exterminated."

"All right," Trixie said. "Honey and I will track him down to his lair; then you can exterminate him."

"Not so fast," Mart cautioned her. "All you girls should do is search for signs. If you discover evidence that a professional poacher is systematically depleting the preserve of game, report to me. I will take over from then on."

"Oh, great," Trixie said sarcastically. "Just great. Then you can wear the feather *we* earned in *your* cap. That will be the day."

A Snare • 15

SCHOOL CLOSED at noon on Wednesday, and Di came home on the bus with the other Bob-Whites. Instead of going home, the Beldens went straight up to the Manor House, where a festive luncheon awaited them.

As they trudged up the driveway, Ben passed them in his flashy lemon-colored convertible. Because it was such a bright, sunshiny day, the top was down, and Trixie could see that the backseat was piled high with cartons of groceries.

"I guess he can be useful, after all," she said to Jim. "He's obviously done the shopping for Miss Trask. I can't believe she trusted him with a list.

Just to be funny, he probably bought ten pounds of salt instead of sugar."

"I doubt that," Jim said easily. "Ben likes to eat, and he knows the stores will be closed until Friday morning. Anyway, I don't think Miss Trask did trust him with a list. She probably phoned the order in, so all he had to do was pick up the cartons."

Honey, Di, and the Belden boys were several yards ahead of them. Jim, as host, was carrying Di's suitcase, and Trixie had trailed behind the others with him.

Jim grinned at her. "I gather that you have recovered from your yen for Ben. I'm sure glad of it, Trix."

Trixie sighed heavily. It would be so comforting if she could just tell Jim about the ring and why she had had to pretend to have a "yen for Ben" and, even more important, tell him about the dead deer.

Although she and Honey, while patrolling that morning and the day before, had searched for signs that there was a poacher in the preserve, they had seen nothing. But that, Trixie felt, was because they had kept to the trails. If there were any clues, she was sure that they could only be found on the paths.

Aloud she asked Jim, "How's the roof on the clubhouse coming along? The radio said this morning that we were going to have a 'white' Thanksgiving."

Jim nodded. "A cold front is on the way from the

Middle West. Unless it swerves farther north or farther south, we're sure to have precipitation—rain, sleet, or snow."

"A blizzard, probably," Trixie said dismally. "Is the roof anywhere near fixed?"

"No," he told her in an equally dismal voice. "It's been quite a job, what with having to repair the wall first. If we get precipitation along with sub-freezing temperatures, we can't do any more work until we get a thaw."

"Everything will be ruined," Trixie wailed. "What can we do, Jim?"

"Plenty," he replied cheerfully. "We boys are going to eat and run at lunch today. We can get a lot done before dark. Even so, there'll still be a rather large gaping hole in the roof, but we can cover it with tarpaulin."

"If there's a high wind," Trixie pointed out, "that won't do any good. The tarpaulin will end up at Mr. Lytell's store."

"Don't be such a pessimist," Jim said. "We may not get anything but a light rain. The only thing that really bothers me, Trix, is Brian's car. Since it was such a super bargain, I imagine the secondhand dealer has already sold it. I feel bad about that. Brian may never get another chance to buy a jalopy like that for fifty bucks. I wish one of us could have done something."

Trixie suddenly began to feel smug. Although she couldn't tell Jim about it, she *had* done something. Maybe everything would work out all right in the end, after all.

Although the luncheon was a gay affair, it was hurried because the Bob-Whites had so much to do. Trixie gobbled her ice cream and raced home to change clothes so she and Honey could do a thorough job of patrolling the preserve on the north side of the road. This time, because darkness was such a long way off, she was going to explore the bypaths for clues.

She had just donned her blue jeans and old sweater when her mother came into the room. "I hope you remember, dear," Mrs. Belden said, "that you promised to keep an eye on Bobby this afternoon while I do the shopping for our party tomorrow."

"Oh, woe," Trixie moaned. "I completely forgot. Honey and I planned to patrol earlier than we usually do."

"Well, I won't be gone long," her mother said. "I just want to pick up a few last-minute things, to make sure they're fresh. As you know, I did the big shopping on Monday." She frowned. "I hate to interfere with your job. I'd take Bobby with me, but you know how restless he gets when I take the time to examine a head of cabbage or a bunch of carrots."

"It's all right, Moms," Trixie said quickly. "Di

and Ben have promised to take care of Bobby for me whenever I have to patrol. Is that all right with you?"

"Certainly," Mrs. Belden said with a smile. "Di, with two sets of twins for brothers and sisters, should be a perfectly competent baby-sitter."

"Good." Trixie dashed downstairs and out to the terrace where Bobby was playing with a small, red fire engine. She grabbed his hand. "Come on. You're going to spend the afternoon up at the Manor House."

He pulled his hand free. "Hey! Whatcha think ya doing? You hurted me, *badly*."

"I didn't, either," Trixie retorted. "But I *am* in a hurry. Come on." She scooped up his red fire engine. "You can play with this up there just as well as you can down here."

"CAN'T!" he yelled. "All my firemen are down here."

Trixie tried to control her impatience. "Well, bring the firemen along, too. Not that I see any."

He gave her a withering look and began to gather up some clothespins that he had dipped into red ink. He put some of them into the fire engine and stuffed the others into the pockets of his jeans. "My men," he announced in a tone of voice that indicated that Trixie was both blind and stupid. "I'm the chief, 'course."

"Oh, I see," Trixie said meekly. "You can put out a lot of fires on the Wheelers' veranda. Ben and Di are going to play with you while Honey and I patrol the preserve. You will be a good boy, won't you, Bobby?"

He tossed his blond, silky curls. "Not a boy. I'm a fire chief!" He led the way up the path, and, when they reached the stable, he ran ahead to throw himself into Regan's arms. "I'm a fire chief, Regan," he yelled. "Hey! You got some fires for me to put out?"

"Why, sure," Regan replied, hoisting the little boy to a seat on his broad shoulders.

Honey had already saddled and bridled Susie and Starlight. She handed the black mare's reins to Trixie and mounted the chestnut gelding. "Di and Ben," she told Trixie, "drove into town to get some stuff Ben forgot this morning. Isn't that typical of him? He brought back everything but the most important items: the turkey and pumpkin pies!"

"Oh," Trixie moaned. "I can't go until they come back. Who'll keep an eye on Bobby?"

"I will," Regan offered good-naturedly. "There's a whole box of crinkly red tissue paper upstairs in my room. It'll make a grand fire, won't it, Bobby?" He set Bobby down astride the little engine and rang the bell.

Starlight shied, and if Honey hadn't been such an excellent horsewoman, she might have fallen off.

"That will teach you," Regan said, frowning up at her. "Sitting there like a sack of meal, with the reins slack! You should know better, Honey Wheeler, and if you don't, it's time you learn."

Honey flushed. "I am getting awfully careless, Regan," she admitted. "It's just that Trixie and I have done so much riding lately that I feel more at home in the saddle than I do in a chair."

"Feel at home as much as you like," he retorted. "But don't forget that a horse is a live animal. A chair isn't. Even the best rider can get thrown and dragged by the gentlest, best-schooled horse in the world." He turned on Trixie the moment she had swung into the saddle. "You've been getting careless lately, too. If you don't remember to keep your heels down, you won't be allowed to ride anything around here except a sawhorse." He grinned suddenly to let them know that he wasn't really cross. "Get going, you two. What are you waiting for—a streetcar?"

They walked their horses down the driveway, and, as soon as they were out of earshot, Trixie said to Honey, "Regan is really so wonderful. I don't know how he stands us. Taking care of Bobby when this is supposed to be his afternoon off, isn't it?"

Honey nodded. "Regan adores Bobby, and, besides, you know how he is about his day off. He usually hangs around here, anyway." They trotted along the edge of Glen Road until they reached Mr. Lytell's store, then turned north into the woods.

"Today," Trixie said firmly, "we're not going to stick to the trails. It won't get dark for another three hours, so we've just got to explore the paths."

"Oh, Trixie," Honey wailed. "Today of all days!"

"What's wrong with today?" Trixie demanded. "Tomorrow I've got to spend most of the time helping Moms. We may even wake up and find ourselves in the midst of a blizzard. If so, we won't be able to go near the paths for days, and our week is up on Saturday. We can't accept fifty dollars from Miss Trask then if we didn't at least *try* to catch the poacher."

"I know; I know," Honey moaned. "But don't you realize, Trix, that we're riding the two new horses, Starlight and Susie? If we get lost, they—"

"Gleeps," Trixie interrupted in dismay. "I should have figured that out this morning, before we patrolled the other side of the preserve on Strawberry and Lady."

"Besides," Honey continued, just as though Trixie hadn't interrupted, "I really don't think there is any poacher."

"Anyway," Trixie went on, just as though *Honey* hadn't said anything, "we're not going to get lost. I've got a compass." She pushed back the sleeve of her sweater and displayed a wrist compass. "See?

It's really Bobby's, but he won't know the diff."

"Bobby's?" Honey stared in amazement. "If it belongs to him, it can't be any good. He breaks just about everything he gets his hands on."

"That's the point," Trixie said, giggling. "And I'm not talking about a point of the compass. Aunt Alicia gave this to Bobby on his birthday, but it cost a lot of money, so Moms has been keeping it for him until he's old enough to take care of it properly."

"Oh," Honey said. "Does your mother know that you borrowed it? Suppose we break it. It would be just our luck."

Trixie grinned. "No, Moms doesn't know I borrowed it. I meant to tell her, but right after I strapped it on my wrist, she came in and reminded me that I was supposed to take care of Bobby this afternoon. That made me forget everything. But she won't mind. I mean, it's been sitting on the mantelpiece for ages, so anybody but Bobby could borrow it. It isn't as though it had been locked up in a safe or something. It's not *that* valuable."

Honey laughed. "Well, just don't fall off Susie and break it. I know Bobby. He doesn't mind breaking his own things, but if anybody else touches them—well, revenge is sweet."

They had reached the clearing at the fork now and stopped their horses. "You take this path," Trixie said, pointing, "and I'll take the one that leads to the spot where I found the dead deer. That's where I think we'll find clues."

"Oh, fine," Honey jeered. "I have no intention of leaving you for one minute. You've got the compass —remember?"

For answer, Trixie unstrapped it and handed it to her. "Okay. Meet you back here in about ten minutes."

But Honey refused to accept the compass. "Not me. I'd be sure to break it. Anyway, I can't read all those queer symbols. Besides, I think you have to know where north is first and face in that direction, don't you?"

"That's easy," Trixie replied. "You're facing north now, because the sunset is on your left."

Honey twisted her head around in a semicircle. "The light seems to be all over the place. That's the trouble with it. It doesn't stay put in one neat little spot. I just don't trust it—or compasses."

"Oh, Honey," Trixie cried impatiently. "The compass is supposed to figure all those things out for you. If you just lay it on a flat rock, the arrow will point to north."

"What good is that going to do me if I get lost?" Honey demanded. "I'd never have the luck to be near a flat rock at that moment. And even if I did, knowing where north is wouldn't do me any good. If I get lost, I certainly want to get back home, not end up somewhere up around the North Pole."

Trixie howled with laughter. "I guess you're right. This compass isn't going to do either of us a bit of good. I can't understand the symbols, either, and I feel just the way you do about north. If we can't travel in a straight line, knowing where the points of the compass are wouldn't do us a bit of good."

"And these paths," Honey agreed emphatically, "do anything but travel in a straight line. Even if we could understand what that compass was trying to tell us, we'd have to get off and lay it on a flat rock every five minutes. Pretty soon it would be too dark to find a rock, let alone read the compass."

Trixie strapped it back on her wrist. "When Bobby's old enough to figure it all out, I hope he explains it to me. Brian and Jim and Mart are over my head when it comes to directions. So I guess we'd better stick together, Honey." She nudged Susie into a walk and led the way along the path that led to the other, smaller clearing.

In a few minutes she stopped and yelled over her shoulder, "Oh, look, Honey. There's all the proof we need."

Starlight edged past Susie into the clearing. "I don't see anything," Honey said, vaguely peering around into the brush.

"Look up, not down," Trixie cried impatiently, pointing. "See that dead rabbit hanging from that sapling? He was caught in a snare. Mart drew a diagram of a rabbit snare for me. A partridge snare, too. If the poacher wanted to catch partridges by the dozen, all he'd have to do is set up snares around the feeding stations. And I'll bet he has!"

The Cabin in the Clearing · 16

HOW HORRIBLE!" Honey gasped. "Daddy will have a fit if anyone has been catching his valuable birds. Do you suppose the poacher has been setting snares for pheasants, too?"

"No," Trixie said. "They can be shot at quite easily because of their bright-colored feathers. But partridges sort of blend into the underbrush, so you can practically step on one before you see it. Then they zoom up suddenly with a *whir-r* of their wings and disappear before the hunter has time to aim."

"Jim has shot lots of partridges," Honey said. "But then, of course, Jim is awfully smart. And I remember he said that you shouldn't really shoot them unless you have a gun dog, because they're so hard to find. That's why he bought a springer spaniel and has spent so much time teaching Patch to retrieve. Jim says unless you hunt with a good retriever, there is apt to be a lot of useless killing of birds, and, worse, a cripple can get away and later die a slow death of misery."

Trixie nodded. "That's one thing about snares. The bird dies quickly and almost painlessly, once he tries to force his way through the noose. He's held a prisoner, too, so his body can't get lost. But anybody who sets a snare usually keeps a close watch on it, because a fox or a catamount can get the bird even before the trapper gets there."

Honey shuddered and said in a scared whisper, "That poacher might be in the thicket right now, listening to every word we say. Let's go, Trixie. He probably has a gun."

And then, as though in proof of her statement, two shots rang out in rapid succession. The blasts were so close by that Susie shied violently. While they had been talking, both girls had let the reins go slack, and almost before they knew it, both horses had bolted and were tearing along the narrow path.

Susie was in the lead, and by the time Trixie did gather up the reins, the horse was out of control. Tree branches slapped Trixie in the face and brought blinding tears of pain to her eyes. She pulled as hard as she could on the curb, yelling, "Whoa! Whoa!" to no avail. Susie flew along as though pursued by a thousand devils. The "devil" in this case was only Starlight, but Trixie guessed that he, too, was panic-stricken. He was following Susie so closely that Trixie knew if the mare suddenly stopped, there would be a terrific collision, and Honey might be badly hurt. Susie showed no signs of even slowing, but she might stumble on a rock, and then both girls would probably be thrown. To make matters worse, the path wound dizzily through the woods so that, instead of galloping in a straight line, Susie kept swerving abruptly, sometimes to the right, sometimes to the left, so that it was hard for Trixie to keep her seat in the saddle. If only Honey, who was so much more experienced a horsewoman, were in the lead!

But, finally, from sheer exhaustion Trixie guessed, Susie gradually slowed from a dead run to a canter and at last to a trot. As the path widened, Starlight came up so that the girls were now riding abreast.

"They're under control now," Honey gasped, her face very white, "but where are we?"

"I haven't the foggiest notion," Trixie got out, panting. "Let's stop and see if Bobby's compass will be of any help."

And then they came around a bend and found

themselves in a large clearing, and, to their amazement, right smack in the middle of it was a rustic cabin. The horses stopped of their own free will, as though they, too, were surprised.

Not far from the cabin was a pit in which were dying embers of a wood fire. Above it hung a black pot, and a mingling of delicious odors from it permeated the air in the clearing.

In an awed silence, the girls dismounted and stared at each other. "Could this be where the poacher lives?" Honey asked.

"I guess so," Trixie said. "But he must have been poaching for a long, long time. That cabin wasn't built in a few days. Look how long it's been taking the boys just to fix the roof of our clubhouse."

They moved over and peered through a window. The interior was neat and clean but sparsely furnished. A bunk was in one corner, and in the center of the room there were two homemade chairs and a table. Hanging from the ceiling near the two windows on the opposite side of the cabin were several thick leatherlike strips about twelve inches long.

"Why, it's pemmican!" Trixie suddenly cried. "I mean, jerked venison. The Indians used to make it into pemmican. It keeps for months like that and doesn't have to be cooked."

"Venison!" Honey cried. "Then those strips must be what's left of that dead deer."

"Maybe," Trixie said. "But I kind of doubt it. That deer is probably still hanging."

With the horses trailing behind them, they went around to the back. "Why, there's a vegetable garden," Trixie cried excitedly. She pointed to some frost-blackened vines. "Tomatoes, pumpkin, squash, and cucumbers. That whole row of flattened tops must be carrots that haven't been dug yet. And there's kale, which can stay out all winter. And look. Over there are beets, turnips, and parsnips. They don't have to be brought in until the weather gets very cold."

"Well, poachers aren't gardeners," Honey said. "At least, I don't think they are."

"They could be," Trixie argued. "Whoever lives here is trespassing on your father's property and killing game. That makes him a poacher."

"Maybe when the horses were running, they carried us clear out of the preserve," Honey suggested.

Trixie shook her head. "They weren't running in a straight line. Remember? That path wound around like a corkscrew. As the crow flies, we can't be very far from the fork in the trail. So we must be still in your father's preserve."

"But where?" Honey demanded. "And, since we're not crows, how do you figure we are going to get back to the trail?"

Trixie giggled. "Bobby's compass will tell us

where north is, and that's the direction we ought to take, but since we can't fly in a straight line, we'll simply have to unwind ourselves."

Honey's lower lip trembled. "I don't know how you can laugh, Trixie. It's getting darker by the minute. You know as well as I do that we're lost, and the poacher who lives here has a gun, and he's probably on his way home now." She swung up on Starlight's back. "Our only hope, Trixie, is to follow the horses' hoofprints while there's still light enough to see." Honey was right, and both girls knew it. She led the way across the clearing and started slowly along the path.

Trixie followed on Susie. After a few minutes, she asked, "Are you following the hoofprints? I don't see any, not even Starlight's."

"There aren't any to be seen," Honey said dismally. "The path is nothing but rocks and pine needles and dead leaves. Even an FBI man couldn't find any kind of print on it."

"Well, at least it's a path," Trixie said, trying to sound cheerful. "If we stick to it, we're bound to end up where we started." But Trixie was worried, too. Only a faint yellowish-green light filtered through the evergreen branches now, and soon there would be no light at all. The path was so narrow you could hardly call it a path—not unless you were traveling on foot in broad daylight.

After a long silence, Honey said, "I think we'd better give the horses their heads."

"I'm not so sure about that," Trixie said. "Maybe we'd better get off and lead the horses. I mean, they must have broken or bruised a lot of branches when they were galloping madly along. But you can't expect horses to know the difference between a bruised branch and one that hasn't been touched. But we should be able to tell the difference."

Honey sniffed, and although Trixie couldn't see her face, she guessed that Honey was very close to tears. "That's what you think," she told Trixie. "Jim and Indians can read all sorts of signs in the woods, like broken branches and all, but you and I can't. Also, it's soon going to be so dark we won't be able to see our hands in front of our faces, let alone read our palms so we can find out whether our lifeline ends here and now."

Trixie laughed. "Even if we are lost, Honey, we're not going to die. I mean, we won't be lost long enough so we'll starve to death."

"I'm starving right now," Honey complained. "I wish we'd had sense enough to eat some of that poacher's stew before we left."

"Hunter's stew is the right word," Trixie said. "It did smell delicious. But don't talk about it. I'm so hungry I could eat raw horsemeat."

Honey suddenly giggled. "That's a thought. If

worse comes to worse, we can kill Starlight and Susie and eat them. But first we'll skin them and keep ourselves warm that way." Her giggle ended in what sounded like a sob. "That will be the day."

"Oh, Honey, don't get discouraged," Trixie pleaded. "Give Starlight his head, and let's trot for a while. He may lead us right back to the fork. It can't be too far from here."

Honey suddenly held up her right hand to show that she was going to stop. "We're at a fork right now. This path you're so crazy about has suddenly become *two* paths."

Trixie stood up in her stirrups and peered over Honey's shoulder. Sure enough, they would have to make up their minds whether they should bear right or left. Taking the wrong turn would undoubtedly mean that they would become hopelessly lost in the labyrinth.

Trixie sank back into her saddle. "Does Starlight seem to have any preference?" she asked weakly. "Don't guide him with the reins. Just touch him with both heels and see what he does."

The chestnut gelding immediately turned his head to the right and began to trot. "He's right," Honey yelled. "Even I can see broken branches on this path. Maybe he doesn't know his way home, but I guess he knows how to get back to the trail. Look at him!"

"Then let's canter," Trixie said. "Whether right is right or wrong, we'd better find out as soon as we can. It's getting darker all the time."

Both of the horses needed little urging to break into a gallop, and that was encouraging. "They wouldn't hurry if they weren't headed back toward the stable," Trixie called to Honey.

And then the corkscrew path suddenly merged with another, and the girls realized gratefully that they were back on one of the main trails. In a few minutes, the trail ended on Glen Road across from Mr. Lytell's store.

Breathing loud sighs of relief, they forced the impatient horses to walk along the road toward the Manor House. "That was close," Honey finally got out. "The boys were right, Trixie. We should never have left the trails."

"We *had* to," Trixie retorted. "And we did get proof that there is a poacher, living in the middle of the preserve."

"What good is that going to do us?" Honey demanded. "We'll never be able to find our way back to that cabin. I feel the same way about it as I did about the dead deer you found on Sunday. It was all a daymare."

Trixie thought for a minute in silence. Honey was right. Since they could not possibly ever find their way back to that cabin in the big clearing, there was no sense in telling the boys about their discovery. Brian and Jim would only scorn them for leaving the trails, then jeeringly sum up their story.

Trixie could just imagine what the boys would say: "You got panicky because you got lost, and imagined the whole business. A cabin and a vegetable garden in the midst of the woods! How wacky can you get?"

Mart, however, might feel differently. He was nowhere near as good a woodsman as Jim was, but he might be able to help them find the poacher's cabin. He would at least know how to read a compass. . . . Compass!

Trixie pushed back the sleeve of her sweater. The wrist compass had disappeared. "Oh, Honey," she gasped. "Bobby's compass! I guess I didn't strap it on very securely, and it must have been brushed off by a branch when the horses ran away with us."

"Oh, *no*," Honey moaned. "Even if we had the money, we couldn't buy him another one until the stores open on Friday."

"That's right," Trixie groaned, all other worries driven from her mind. "And you know Bobby. Years might go by without his even remembering that he owns a compass. But now that I've lost it, he'll be sure to want to show it to somebody at our party tomorrow."

Help From Mart • 17

TRIXIE'S DIRE PREDICTION came true sooner than she expected. When she brought Bobby home after she and Honey had finished grooming the horses, he burst into the house yelling, "Hey, Mummy. I *have* to have my compass. Ben's going to take me 'sploring tomorrow. Him and Di and me saw a funny-looking bird this afternoon, and we're going to 'splore after it and maybe catch it alive and sell it to a zoo for a billion dollars. It looks sort of like a parrot but mostly like a squirrel, but, on account of Ben isn't as smart as Jim, we might get losted, so I *have* to have my compass."

Trixie grabbed his plump arm. "You won't have

time to go exploring tomorrow, Bobby," she said in a whisper. "You know perfectly well that it's Thanksgiving, and also you know there's no such thing as a bird that looks like a squirrel. Come on. I'll tell you a story while you take a bath."

He yanked away from her. "Is so a bird that looks like a squirrel. I saw it my own self. It was sitting on a small, little, teeny-weeny bush, and Ben gave me some salt to put on its tail, but when I got so close, it flewed away into the woods." He demonstrated with his fat hands how close he had gotten.

Mrs. Belden, who had been grating raw carrots into a big wooden salad bowl, joined in the conversation then. "If you got that close, Bobby," she said with a laugh, "why did you bother with salt? You could have grabbed it by the tail. That is, if it had the long bushy tail of a squirrel."

"Didn't," he informed her gravely. "Had a little, teeny-weeny, feathery tail like a chicken."

"Oh, my goodness!" Trixie exploded impatiently. "It's just one of Ben's silly jokes, Bobby. He's always rigging up things like that with strings and a pulley. Remember that 'ghost' he tried to scare Honey with last time he visited her? Even you weren't fooled by it."

"Not a ghost," he stormed. "It's a bird, and we're gonna catch it early tomorrow morning. So I *have* to have my compass. I promised Ben."

"Very well," Mrs. Belden said. "If you promised Ben that he could wear your compass, you shall have it."

Trixie collapsed on the kitchen stool. "He can't, Moms. I borrowed it this afternoon and—and lost it!"

Mrs. Belden stared at her in amazement while Bobby burst into screams of rage. Trixie alternated between covering her face and her ears with her hands. Finally Mrs. Belden led Bobby away, and in a few minutes his howls finally subsided into low sobs.

Mart came into the kitchen then, and while Trixie finished making the salad, she blurted out the whole story. At first he seemed more interested in Bobby's lost compass than he was in the mysterious cabin in the clearing.

"Gleeps, Trix," he said, "you should know better than to touch anything that belongs to Bobby. You won't hear the end of this until you're old and gray."

"It's all Ben's fault," Trixie stormed. "Why did he have to go and rig up that crazy thing?"

Mart wiggled his eyebrows at her. "When you're Bobby-sitting, I have discovered, your imagination is apt to run wild. If you don't keep him amused when he thinks he's a fire chief, you may find yourself in the midst of a holocaust. But fear not, sis. I may be able to pour oil on the troubled waters by lending the lad my own wrist compass. That is, if you'll do me a favor."

"I'll do anything," Trixie said hastily, "if you can keep Moms from looking at me as though she thought I were a thief."

"Pooh," said Mart airily. "So far as our maternal parent is concerned, you are already forgiven, since you immediately confessed your crime. She may have a few well-chosen words to say to you on the subject later, but that will be that. Once Bobby is all sunny smiles again, the thing will soon be forgotten. Since I am the one who can produce those smiles, I will now dictate the terms. I will lend him my wrist compass on this condition: You tell me here and now why you asked Dad to get that diamond ring out of the bank. I am not a member of the feline family, but curiosity is slowly but surely killing me."

"Oh, all right," Trixie said crossly. "But you've got to promise to keep it a secret."

Mart made an elaborate gesture of crossing his heart. Then Trixie began at the very beginning. Before she was halfway through, Mart threw his arms around her and hugged her so tightly that she couldn't breathe.

"You super-stupendous lame-brain," he cried happily. "How do you do it? You always give the impression that you're totally insane, and yet, in the end, you're the only one who makes sense." He danced around the kitchen with her until Trixie tapped him on the head with the vegetable grater.

"Listen, muttonhead," she said, gasping for breath, "it's not as simple as you seem to think. There *is* a poacher in the preserve. We can't collect our salary as gamekeepers on Saturday if we don't do something about him first."

Mart immediately sobered and collapsed on the kitchen stool. "True," he agreed. "But your cabin-in-the-clearing story is so fantastic, I can't believe a word of it. But first things must come first. Right now I shall go upstairs and pour oil on the troubled waters of Bobby's anguished sobs. While I am doing so, Moms will undoubtedly seize that opportunity to explain to you the meaning of the Shakespearean quotation: 'Never a borrower nor a lender be.' Then you must bathe and don suitable garments so that I can escort you up to the Manor House, where a festive repast awaits us. En route, we can discuss the poacher problem and what to do about it."

Trixie tapped him again on the head with the grater. "I supppose *you* don't have to shower and change. And what about Brian? Is he going to dine at the Wheelers' in the same dirty clothes I last saw him in?"

"Brian," Mart informed her, "is showering at the home of our host and hostess and is wearing a handsome suit belonging to Jim."

"Oh, fine," Trixie said sarcastically. "Somebody had better tell Brian the facts of life about what happens to borrowers. He and Jim are getting to be so chummy that it's boring. Brian never comes home to change anymore. Why doesn't he just move up there bag and baggage? Then Moms can rent his room and hire somebody to do his chores."

Mart gurgled. "Our elder sibling, commonly known as Brian Belden, has been doing his household chores at the crack of dawn every morning so that he can devote all of the daylight hours to work on the clubhouse. I have, too, as you would know if you did not stagger off to the stable every A.M. with both eyes tightly closed."

He darted out of the kitchen, and Trixie hastily began to collect china and silver so she could set the table for her parents and Bobby. Mrs. Belden joined her.

"Trixie, honey," she said, folding paper napkins, "you shouldn't have borrowed Bobby's compass. I know that you didn't mean to lose it, but you realize, don't you, that you'll have to buy him another one as soon as you can?"

Wordlessly, and very shamefacedly, Trixie nodded her head. "I'm sorry," she gulped.

"All right," her mother said. "There's no real rush about it, because it's far too expensive a thing for him to treat as a toy, anyway. Now, run along and get ready for dinner at the Wheelers'. None of you can stay late. Tomorrow is going to be a very busy day. Although the ham and turkeys are already cooked, there are going to be a lot of last-minute things for you to do." She frowned worriedly. "I don't want to interfere with your job, but couldn't Mart patrol the preserve tomorrow with Honey so you can help me?"

"I'm sure he will," Trixie said meekly. "I'll ask him right away." She fled upstairs.

Mart agreed, and later, as they climbed the path to the Manor House, he said, "I fully planned to do some patrolling on my own tomorrow, anyway. If Honey goes with me, all the better, because she can show me how to get to that house in the clearing."

"Not a prayer," Trixie said. "I keep trying to tell you, we have no idea where we were. It was sheer luck that we're still not in the labyrinth." They had reached the wooded section that lay between the path and the stable. The overhanging branches of the trees cut off the light from the crescent moon, and they turned on their flashlights. "But she can show you that rabbit snare. And we did hear two shots, Mart. We couldn't both have imagined them. Besides, that's what made the horses run away."

"Horses do not have vivid imaginations," Mart

agreed. "And they also probably blazed a trail to the big clearing. I'm not the woodsman Jim is, but I'll bet I can follow the bruised and broken branches along that narrow path."

"I doubt it," Trixie said. "Don't forget the storm broke and bruised a lot of branches, too."

"Maybe we ought to tell Jim," Mart said. "The roof has reached the stage where he and Brian don't need me anymore, but if Jim has to quit to track down a poacher, I don't think the work will be finished before we get heavy snow."

"That's the point," Trixie said. "So you've got to find that cabin. Then all you have to do is tell Jim so he can report it to the game protector. What happens to poachers? Do they go to jail?"

Mart shrugged. "I don't know, but he'll surely have to pay a fine. He sounds like an illegal squatter, too. How do you like that? A house and garden and every little thing on somebody else's property! The nerve of the guy. In fact, I just don't believe anybody has that much nerve. And why didn't Fleagle discover him?"

"His horse didn't run away with him," Trixie said. "That's the answer. Fleagle was lazy, you know. He didn't cover every inch of the preserve when he patrolled. You can count on the fact that he stuck to the trails."

They were on the moonlit driveway now, and she

handed her flashlight to Mart. "Keep this in your jacket pocket for me, please. I'll be sure to forget it. Last time I—"

"Hey," he suddenly interrupted. "You're wearing the diamond ring now. How come?"

"It's a phony," Trixie replied, and explained. "I have to wear it tomorrow, you know, or Dad and Moms will be suspicious."

Mart nodded. "I'm none too happy about the fact that you're deceiving them, but I guess it's a justifiable crime."

"It's no crime to wear an imitation diamond ring," Trixie argued. "And if Moms and Dad should get suspicious and ask me questions, I wouldn't tell any lies. I just hope they don't, that's all."

"Well," Mart said with a chuckle, "when you're old and gray, you must tell them the whole story. They'll enjoy it. As a matter of fact, I have a sneaking suspicion that they'd enjoy it right now. They're awfully good sports, you know."

"That's true," Trixie agreed. "But I've never tested them with a diamond ring before. Moms, thank goodness, didn't seem too mad at me for borrowing Bobby's compass. It's sort of the same thing. After all, I didn't deliberately lose it, and I haven't lost the ring."

"You'll lose it if you don't fork over fifty bucks to Mr. Lytell on Saturday," Mart pointed out. "He has a perfect right to sell it to someone and give you the difference."

"Don't rub it in," Trixie moaned. "That's why we've got to earn our salary as gamekeepers, and that means exterminating that poacher."

"I'll do my best tomorrow morning," Mart promised.

They hurried inside the big house, where the others were waiting for them. Because they were going to the Beldens' party tomorrow, Miss Trask had decided to have a Thanksgiving feast that evening. Thus the cook could have the next day off, and, as Miss Trask said, "This is a very good thing, because ever since Celia left, Cook has been getting crosser by the minute."

"Have you heard from Celia recently?" Trixie asked Miss Trask. "Are she and Tom still in Canada?"

"I don't know where they are," Miss Trask replied worriedly. "I got one of those 'wish you were here' postcards yesterday from them both, and it was mailed from Montreal. But that doesn't mean anything. Tom took his longbow with him, so I know he plans to do some deer hunting upstate before they return. He took his thirty-thirty rifle, too, so he could hunt in counties where shooting with a rifle is permissible. It all adds up to this," she finished in a discouraged tone of voice: "Tom is going to keep on trying to get a deer until the very last minute. If we have a blizzard between now and the weekend, they may be delayed for several days."

"We just can't have a blizzard," Honey wailed. "On account of the clubhouse, Miss Trask. But don't you worry about a thing. Now that I don't have to go to school, I can help a lot around the house. I can do everything that Celia did, and, don't forget, I can cook, too."

Her cousin Ben hooted with laughter. "You cook! I'd rather eat a raw frog."

Trixie glared at him across the table. "I'll have you know," she informed him tartly, "that Honey is a very good cook. And so am I, in case you're interested."

He raised his eyebrows in pretended astonishment and asked Brian, "Can either of them—"

To Trixie's amazement, Brian suddenly became protective. "Boil water without burning it?" he finished for Ben. "The answer is yes, they can. Can you?"

Ben flushed. "Ah, I was only kidding," he said sheepishly. "I didn't mean anything."

Mart said easily, "You'd be surprised to know how well our siblings can cook." He kicked Trixie under the table. "Hunter's stew made with venison is their specialty."

Honey gulped and said, "Oh, Ben knows how to

make a hunter's stew. He learned how at camp. Didn't you, Ben?"

"Not really," he replied, laughing. "I know what to put into the pot, but after that my mind becomes a blank."

Jim, who had been sullenly silent until then, suddenly growled, "People who live in glass houses shouldn't throw stones. Trixie and Honey are better cooks than the one we have now," he told Ben. "If you'd rather eat raw frogs, why don't you scram?"

"Oh, for heaven's sake," Di put in. "Must we all quarrel every time we get together? Ben didn't mean to be critical, Jim. He was only joking."

It was Jim's turn to look sheepish. "I'm sorry," he said to Miss Trask. "I'm not a very good host."

Honey, in that very tactful way of hers, broke the icy silence. "Did you say ghost, Jim?" she inquired sweetly.

Everyone laughed, and from then on things went smoothly.

After the feast, the boys and girls trailed across the hall to the library, where Di and Ben immediately began to play country records. Honey slipped out, beckoning for Trixie to follow. She led the way into her father's den and closed the door.

"Well," she whispered loudly, "what happened about Bobby and the compass? I've been dying of suspense. When you and Mart were so late arriving, I began to think that Bobby had drawn and quartered you."

"Not quite," Trixie said, grinning. She brought Honey up to date on events and finished with, "Bobby's mad at me, all right, but if Ben amuses him with that phony bird tomorrow, he'll probably forget about me. The important thing is for you and Mart to try to find that cabin in the clearing."

Honey shook her head. "Things keep on getting more and more involved. Since Mart has given his compass to Bobby, he and I will surely get lost. But you're the one I'm worried most about."

"Why?" Trixie asked. "I'll be safe at home making potato salad and coleslaw."

"Because of Bobby," Honey hissed. "Have you forgotten the motto Mart gave him months ago? 'Revenge is sweet. *Saccharine*-sweet!' "

Thanksgiving • 18

IN SPITE OF storm warnings and Honey's grim predictions, Thanksgiving was a wonderful day. The sun shone brightly in a cloudless, powder blue sky, and by noon the temperature had risen to a record-breaking seventy-two degrees.

Mart and Honey did not get lost, but neither did they find the cabin in the clearing. Bobby spent the whole morning with Ben and Di and returned triumphantly at lunchtime with his strange bird.

"I shot it my own self and with my bow an' arrow," he announced proudly, "and I 'trieved it my own self 'cause Patch wouldn't."

"I don't blame Patch," said Mr. Belden, looking

at the strange object that Ben had put together, using a moth-eaten stuffed squirrel and the head of an equally moth-eaten stuffed parrot, which he had obviously bought from a taxidermist in town. "This object is neither fur nor feathers, and no self-respecting spaniel would be caught dead with it."

"Nobody was caught dead with it," Bobby yelled. "I caught him dead all by my own self."

"Very smart of you, too," Mrs. Belden said soothingly. "Now you must eat your lunch, Bobby, and take a nice long nap. We're having a party today, so you may stay up later this evening than usual. But you must have a nap."

"Won't," he stormed. "I'm a hunter. Hunters don't take naps."

"Oh, yes, they do, Little Hiawatha," said Mart, lifting Bobby onto the kitchen stool. "Let's 'peetend' this bowl of vegetable soup is hunter's stew, and you made it your own self. Out of that par-squirrel you shot, or should we call it a squirrel-par?"

Bobby, all dimples now, ate hungrily and went off to bed willingly.

Mart really is wonderful with kids, Trixie thought. *I wish I had his patience.*

From then on, she was so busy she forgot all of her worries, and the first guest arrived while she was still dressing. It was so warm that Trixie hated to wear a sweater and skirt, but she knew it would grow much cooler after sundown and that she would be in and out of doors receiving guests until the last one arrived. Hastily she clasped Di's necklace around her throat, slipped on Honey's "diamond" ring, and raced down the stairs to help her mother.

The first arrival, she saw from the hall, was Mr. Lytell. It would never do for him to see her with another "diamond" ring. He would be sure to make comments in that nosy way of his! And the trouble with "party" skirts was that there were no pockets in them.

In a panic, Trixie yanked the ring off her finger and dropped it into a brass bowl on the nearby butterfly table. "As Bobby would say," she told herself, "I'll 'trieve it as soon as Mr. Lytell leaves."

But just then Miss Trask arrived and promptly offered to help serve food and punch. Mrs. Belden gratefully accepted the offer, and so, of course, Mr. Lytell followed Miss Trask into the dining room, hovering at her elbow.

Trixie had always suspected that Mr. Lytell was in love with Miss Trask, and now she knew it. "He'll never leave until she leaves," she moaned to Honey around five o'clock. "And you know Miss Trask. She'll stay on and help with the dishes if she thinks we need her. Can't you get rid of her so I can wear my ring?" She giggled nervously. "I mean, *your* ring, Honey!"

Honey smiled. "Nobody's going to notice that you're not wearing it, Trixie. There must be five million people here. I'll bet you could go around with a ring in your nose like a Fiji Islander, and your parents would never know the difference."

It was eight o'clock before the crowd began to thin. Brian and Mart, who had been supervising the parking and departure of cars, came in then, ravenously hungry. Miss Trask, with Mr. Lytell still hovering at her elbow, served them huge platters of food.

As the boys moved away from the table, Brian said to Trixie, "Hey, squaw. Bring me some hot buttered rolls."

Trixie, hot, tired, and cross, clenched her fist and shook it under his nose. "Get 'em yourself, Sitting Bull."

He grabbed her wrist with his free hand. "Why the naked little fingers?" he demanded. Trixie knew that he was just as hot and tired and cross as she was, but she jerked away from him, and the food on his plate slid off onto the floor. Reddy promptly appeared from nowhere, grabbed a turkey leg, nosed open the screen door to the terrace, and disappeared into the darkness.

"Gleeps," Mart yelled. "Those bones will kill him." He dashed off in pursuit of the red setter, and Brian glared angrily at Trixie.

"Can't you ever do anything without causing

trouble?" he demanded. "After all that fuss about your silly old diamond ring, why aren't you wearing it?"

Out of the corner of one eye, Trixie saw that Mr. Lytell had heard every word. He had been bending over Miss Trask's chair at the other end of the table, but now he straightened. If he had been a dog, Trixie decided, his ears would have pricked up with interest.

"Answer me," Brian was saying irritably. "Why aren't you wearing your ring?"

"Because I lost it in the potato salad," Trixie retorted. "Di's father ate it, and he seems to be still alive, so I'm not going to worry about Reddy and a few turkey bones. He's been swiping them for years."

Brian, his good nature immediately restored, burst into loud laughter. "Are you trying to tell me that Mr. Lynch, one of the richest men in North America, has been swiping diamond rings for years? Or were you referring to Reddy's thieving habits?" He took his hand from Trixie's wrist and gave her an affectionate hug. "Clean up the mess I spilled, like a good girl, and I won't ask you any more embarrassing questions."

Trixie pushed him away from her. "Clean it up yourself. If you only knew it, Brian Belden, I've already done more than enough for you as it is."

She fled out to the terrace, straight into the arms of Ben Riker.

"Say," he said when they had laughingly disentangled themselves, "that kid brother of yours is cute. The trouble with me is that I'm an only child. I've learned a lot this week from hanging around you Beldens and Jim and Honey. And Di, too. You guys are always so busy, you don't have time for practical jokes. I realize now that they're kid stuff. Why, even Bobby knows better. He's more fun than a barrel of monkeys. I wish my mother would adopt him."

"He *is* cute," Trixie said, deciding that she did like Ben Riker, after all. He had improved a lot during the last few days. Instead of being silly, he had actually been helpful in many ways. "Where is Bobby?" she asked suddenly. "I haven't seen him for simply hours. It's time he went up to bed."

"I haven't seen him since he ate a whole bowl of potato chips, single-handed, around seven o'clock," Ben said with a grin. "Weighted down as he was, he couldn't have gone far. I'll collect him and put him to bed for you. That would be fun."

"Gee, thanks," Trixie said, collapsing on the low stone wall of the terrace. "If I don't get my own weight off my feet soon, my ankles will snap in two."

"Consider your baby-sitting problems solved," he

said and went inside through the kitchen door.

Trixie lay flat on her back and stared up at the moon. The temperature had dropped only a few degrees after sundown. Not a breeze was stirring, and it was ominously warm. If that cold front that was moving eastward hit this area, anything could happen, from thunder and lightning to a blizzard. No wonder Brian was so irritable. He and Jim had been working like slaves on the clubhouse, which they could have finished today if it hadn't been for the party. Jim had kept on working until it was too dark to see, but Brian had had to quit early in order to help Mart direct traffic. It must have been frustrating to stand around all afternoon and evening telling people where to park their cars so they could get out whenever they wanted to leave and at the same time not ruin any of Mrs. Belden's flowers.

"Oh, well," Trixie reflected, "I didn't have any fun today, either. What with worrying about that darn old ring!" She closed her eyes wearily and fell asleep almost instantly. A second later, or so it seemed, Ben was shaking her.

"I tell you he's gone," he was whispering hoarsely. "I've searched the house and the grounds. There isn't a sign of him."

"Who—what?" Trixie sat up, rubbing her eyes.

"Bobby," he hissed. "I don't think we ought to frighten your mother, but we've got to do something.

I remember now he said something to me about the brook. But he couldn't have gone down there in the pitch-dark, could he, Trixie?"

"Oh, no," Trixie gasped. "He has a flashlight of his own. He could do *anything.*" Just then Honey and Di came out on the terrace. Brian and Jim followed them. "Bobby's disappeared," Trixie wailed. "Don't let Moms know. Get all the flashlights you can find—and—" She burst into tears.

"Whoa," Brian said steadily. "He's probably sound asleep under his bed." He raced indoors.

"That's right," Honey said soothingly. "You've forgotten, Trixie. On warm nights, Bobby always sleeps under his bed."

Trixie immediately stopped crying. "Did you look under his bed, Ben?"

He shook his head. "I never thought of that."

Mart appeared then with Reddy at his heels. "I had to search the whole four acres," he complained, frowning at Trixie, "and finally found him down at the brook, licking his chops."

"Oh, never mind about Reddy," Trixie cried. "Bobby's disappeared. At least, I think he has."

At that moment, Brian came back with several flashlights. "He's nowhere indoors. We'll have to search every inch of our property. I'll start with the brook."

"Wait a minute," Mart said, and the freckles stood

out in the whiteness of his face. "Are you sure Bobby isn't in the house?"

"Positive," Ben and Brian said in unison.

"Well, he isn't anywhere on our property," Mart said. "Including the brook. I just combed it all, inch by inch, trying to find Reddy."

"The Wheelers' lake," Trixie gasped. "He couldn't have gone up there. He *couldn't* have!"

"Take it easy," Jim said, taking a flashlight from Brian. "Come on with me, Trixie. It's all very simple. Bobby has run away again for some reason. If he isn't down here, he's up at our house or in Regan's apartment over the garage."

"But nobody's home at your place," Trixie objected. "He wouldn't stay there alone."

Jim grabbed her hand and started off toward the path. "Sure he would. Patch is there. They're probably curled up together on a sofa, sound asleep." He added over one shoulder to the others, "The rest of you may as well come along, too, just in case we have to search the whole house. But my guess is that we'll find him in less than five minutes."

Too Good to Be True • 19

BUT THEY DIDN'T. Even after they had all searched the big house, the stable, and the garage, there was no sign of Bobby.

"I guess the boathouse is the next step," Mart said reluctantly. "Let's go, men. You girls check up on the clubhouse."

The boys started off in one direction, Di and Honey in another, but Trixie stood rooted to the spot. Her legs were trembling so she couldn't move. *It's all my fault*, she thought miserably. *I was supposed to keep an eye on him, and he probably ran away to get back at me because I lost his compass.*

No, that wasn't like Bobby. He only ran away when he himself had committed some crime. What crime had he committed? Trixie stood alone in the Wheelers' kitchen and tried to think. Eating a whole bowl of potato chips wasn't a crime in Bobby's eyes. Bowl! That was the answer, of course. The brass bowl on the butterfly table. She herself, without thinking, had hurriedly dumped a big box of potato chips into it earlier that day. Bobby must have found the ring at the bottom. This provided him with a golden opportunity for revenge. He had no way of knowing that it was only a cheap imitation, and so he had probably gone off somewhere in order to hide it in some safe place. Bobby was forever hiding things in "a safe place" and then forgetting where the place was. A good safe place in this case might be at the bottom of the lake.

Trixie shuddered. She could almost see him poised on the edge of a slippery rock in the moonlight . . . and nobody near enough to hear the splash and his cries of "Holp! Holp!"

"No, no," she told herself fiercely. "Bobby would take my ring and hide it, but he wouldn't deliberately throw it away. He went off to hide it and then got so tired he fell asleep at the very spot. But where?"

All of a sudden, Trixie thought she knew the answer. She grabbed a flashlight and raced off up the path to the red trailer. And there she found him, curled up on one of the bunks with Patch lying at his feet.

"Bobby, Bobby," she cried, gathering him into her arms. "Don't ever do this again. You've scared us almost to death."

He opened his eyes and, hugging her tightly, immediately began to whimper. "Trixie, I tookted your ring and losted it. I didn't mean to. It just slipped out of my hands, sort of, down the drainpipe. Mummy's going to be awful mad at me 'cause I can't never, never sell my squirrel-bird for enough money to buy you another one. So I runned away."

From sheer relief, Trixie was crying herself now. "It's all right, Bobby darling," she crooned. "The ring was only worth a dollar, and you don't have to buy me another one. Stop crying, and I'll tell you a secret."

"A see-crud?" He was all smiles now, twisting and wriggling delightedly. "An honest-to-goodness see-crud, Trix?"

"That's right," she told him. "But you must promise not to tell Brian. Or Jim. Or Daddy and Moms. You can tell Mart and Honey, but nobody else. Promise?"

He nodded his blond head solemnly.

"Well," she said, still holding him close, "I gave the real ring to Mr. Lytell so he wouldn't sell that car Brian wants so much. You know the one. It was sort of a swap, like the Aladdin story in the *Arabian Nights.* Remember? Old lamps for new. I don't care anything about the real ring even, but Brian does care an awful lot about the car. It's going to be a surprise, see? So you mustn't tell him."

And then Trixie felt rather than heard someone coming up the trailer steps. She whirled around, and there was Brian. The expression on his face was one of utter amazement, and at first she thought it was because he had not really dared to hope that he might find Bobby in the *Robin.* But when he spoke, she realized that while he had been walking silently along the pine-needle carpet of the path, he must have heard her sharing the secret with Bobby. Wordlessly he took the little boy out of her arms and hugged him as tightly as she had hugged him. After what seemed like a long silence, he said, "I don't know whether to brain you or bless you, Trixie." He left the trailer and hoisted Bobby to his broad shoulders.

Trixie followed them slowly down the path toward the stable. "Oh, don't be mad, Brian," she pleaded. "I don't care anything about that silly old ring."

"Mad?" he asked in a low voice. "Of course I'm mad, you lame-brained idiot. Mad with joy."

Jim suddenly joined them then, appearing out of

the woods. In the same low voice Brian had used, he said, "Well, I see the lost is found." He reached up and gently tugged one of Bobby's silky curls.

"That's right," Brian said huskily. "And the mad female who found him has also fixed things so that Mr. Lytell didn't sell that jalopy, after all. You tell Jim about it, Trix. I can't. I seem to be all choked up, as though I were coming down with a cold."

"I couldn't seem to talk, either," Trixie told Honey the next morning as they cantered along the trail. "All of a sudden, I felt as though I had some of Bobby's pet frogs in my throat, so, in the end, he was the one who told Jim about it. It was an awfully garbled version, of course, with a lot of talk about old lamps and new lamps, but Jim caught on right away. He bopped me over the head with his flashlight and stalked off into your house."

Honey laughed. "You should have heard what he said to me about it, Trix. He thinks you're just about the most wonderful girl in the whole wide world, and so do I."

"Don't be ridic," Trixie said. "I'm a moron. But just to prove that I'm not really, I'm going to find our way back to that cabin in the clearing. I've figured it all out. Instead of starting at the fork, we'll start from the spot on the trail where the path merged into it. And this is it."

"How smart you are," Honey cried admiringly. "Instead of winding our way through the labyrinth, all we have to do is go back along this path in reverse. I mean, turn left at that little fork where Starlight turned right. We can't possibly go wrong, and in just a few minutes we'll be in the big clearing."

"No sooner said than done," Trixie said, starting Strawberry off at a canter. And, sure enough, five minutes later she reined her horse to a stop a few yards from the cabin. Honey pulled Lady to a stop beside her. And then both girls almost fell off their horses.

The door to the cabin opened, and out came Mr. Maypenny!

"Well, now, hello," he said pleasantly. "Real sociable of you to call." He pointed a gnarled finger at Trixie. "You're the Belden girl, unless I miss my guess. I've seen you around, trespassing on my property, and asked Lytell who you were." He chuckled. "Lytell 'lowed as how you were all right, but sort of harum-scarum. No harm in you, though, he says." He took a wrist compass from the pocket of his khaki knickers and held it up so Trixie could see what it was. "Did you happen to drop this compass the day before Thanksgiving when you were moseying around here?"

Trixie slid weakly out of the saddle. "I sure did,"

she said. "But, Mr. Maypenny, this isn't your property." She nodded toward Honey. "This is Honey Wheeler. All of these woods belong to her father. It's part of his huge game preserve."

To Trixie's amazement, he moved closer and shook hands with Honey. "Well, now, I've seen you around, too, and I know your father. A real nice gentleman; a bit stubborn when he chooses to be, but pleasant."

Honey couldn't help smiling as she dismounted. "But I don't understand," she said. "Mr. Lytell told me that you owned land around here, but I didn't think it was in the middle of Daddy's preserve."

"Sure is," he said with a broad grin. "Right smack in the middle of it. A pie-shaped section consisting of ten acres. It's belonged to me and my family for nigh onto a hundred years. Good land, too. I've lived off it, man and boy, since I was your age. Mr. Wheeler, he knows it's good land, too. Offered me a fancy price for it, but, of course, I just laughed. What good would twenty thousand dollars do me if I didn't have a house and garden and plenty of fish and game? Grow my own vegetables, I do. Store some in a root cellar and can others. Dry out some of the meat and can some. Just finished canning a dozen jars of venison stew. Real tasty. There's still plenty in the pot. If you'll come inside and sit down, I'll dish you up some."

In a stunned silence, the girls looped the reins of their horses around branches of a tree and followed him into the cabin. Trixie liked Mr. Maypenny, but she felt that she had been cheated out of a mystery.

Finally Trixie could keep quiet no longer and said, "Well, you're a trespasser. Every time you leave your property or go back to it, you have to trespass on Mr. Wheeler's property."

He shook his head. "There's a law about that to protect property owners. Now Mr. Wheeler, he got real angry when I laughed at his offer of a thousand dollars an acre. Said he was going to block up the paths and trails so I'd be penned up like a bull in a fenced pasture. I kept on laughing and told him to talk to his lawyer. Next day he came back, real meeklike and humble, and offered me twenty thousand dollars for the land." The old man, chuckling reminiscently, ladled the delicious-smelling stew into earthenware bowls.

Honey giggled. "I wish I'd been there. Daddy—meek! It must have been a riot. He's so used to buying anything he wants." She tasted the stew. "Yummy-yum. It's divine, Mr. Maypenny. I wish you were cook at our house. The one we've got now is just terrible. Nothing has any flavor."

"Well, now," Mr. Maypenny said, sitting on the bunk, "a stew just isn't worth putting into a pot unless you put everything in your garden in it. In that I got turnips and parsnips and carrots and potatoes and beans and corn. And I don't use any water a-tall. Why should I? Onions and cabbage and tomatoes are full of water—the right kind of water. I must have used a peck of tomatoes in that goo-lash. Spices, too. I'm a bit heavy with garlic and basil and thyme. There may be some folks who don't go for such, but it suits me to a tee."

Trixie had been eating steadily and now felt less disgruntled. "It suits me, too," she said, grinning. "But, Mr. Maypenny, you've been setting snares for rabbits. That's illegal, even on your own property."

"No, ma'am," he replied pleasantly but emphatically. "Rabbits is varmints. The little robbers would get everything in my garden before I did if I didn't catch 'em first. I got a license to trap 'em. Coon and fox, too. There's a bounty all year round on fox pelts. I trap otter and mink, too, because they go after the trout in my section of the stream. With the money I get for the skins, I buy what I can't grow. Sugar, salt, canned milk, coffee, tea, and such. I don't need a lot, so I don't trap a lot. Personally I like the little critters, but they'd eat me out of house and home if I didn't discourage 'em."

Honey scraped her bowl clean and said, "Mr. Maypenny, Daddy will be home tomorrow. He's going to spend the whole weekend trying to get a deer. If he does get one, will you please show our cook how to make this stew?"

"Better than that," he said. "I got plenty of venison left from the deer I shot with my longbow on Sunday. I aim to pot some of it in a day or so. I'll just pot double the amount. Half for you folks and half for me. I'll put some up in jars for you, too, if you'll bring me the jars. I like to be friendly with my neighbors, though I don't get time to see much of 'em." He chuckled. "Your paw and I could be good friends if he weren't so derned muleheaded stubborn. Told him he could shoot over my property so long as he gave me notice. He seemed pleased, because it's sort of hard to tell exactly where the boundary lines are."

Trixie suddenly remembered something. "Mr. Maypenny," she asked, "is there a crazy person loose in these woods?"

Honey gasped and covered her mouth with both hands. "I forgot all about that. He is crazy, Mr. Maypenny, because he rides around on a unicycle. Trixie saw the tracks."

The old man shook with silent laughter. "I'm your lunatic, girls. Those tracks were left by my deer-carrier. It's a one-wheeled contraption and mighty handy. I'm not as young as I used to be. Get sort of tuckered out if I tote a deer carcass more than a mile or so." He led them outdoors and around to the back where the deer-carrier was parked. It looked like a huge supermarket basket that had been attached to a bicycle wheel.

"Daddy would love having one of those," Honey cried admiringly. "It's wonderful!"

Mr. Maypenny sniffed. "Matt Wheeler is just a boy. If he can't tote his own game, his bow and arrow should be taken away from him. A likeable lad, but what he doesn't know about how to run a game preserve would fill a library." He frowned, sucking in his lips. "That Fleagle! Do you mean to stand there, Honey Wheeler, and tell me your paw paid that man good money? Why, that redheaded adopted brother of yours, Jim Frayne, has more sense in his little finger!"

Honey gasped again. "Do you know Jim, Mr. Maypenny? I mean, does Jim know about your property here in the woods?"

"Imagine so," the old man said easily. "Stopped in real sociablelike the other day when he and that Belden boy were out fixing up the bird-feeding stations that were knocked down by the storm. Gave 'em a few hints that they found helpful, or so they said."

Trixie and Honey stared at each other. Then they both hugged each other, almost hysterical with laughter. "It all comes from keeping see-cruds," Trixie finally managed to murmur.

Honey turned and slipped her arm through Mr.

Maypenny's. "You," she told him pleadingly, "could be the answer to all of our problems. Please, please, say yes, you will."

"Well, now, girl," he said with a pleased expression on his weatherbeaten face, "it would take a stronger man than I am to refuse you anything. If you'd just tell me what you're talking about."

Honey merely winked. "You know perfectly well what I'm talking about, Mr. Maypenny. You're the only man in the whole wide world who should be the gamekeeper for Daddy's preserve. He would engage you tomorrow if Jim and I told him that you would accept."

He winked back at her with such a droll expression on his face that Trixie burst into laughter. "Well, now," he said, laughing as hard as she was, "I sort of got the impression that you kids were the gamekeepers. Wouldn't want to cut you out of any money."

"Oh, no," Honey cried. "On account of school and all, we can't work after this weekend. We only did it because there wasn't anybody else, and besides, we had to have the money."

Both talking at once, they told him the whole story then. When he heard about Trixie's ring and Brian's car, and the clubhouse, he threw up his hands. "Why, it's like something out of a book," he chortled. "If ever a bunch of kids needed help, it's you all. But I must say I admire you for carrying on by yourselves."

"We tried," Trixie said forlornly. "But if you don't think we deserve that fifty dollars tomorrow, we won't accept it."

He frowned at her. "Never said anything of the kind. In my opinion, you've done a grand job. Why, Fleagle would never have noticed those single-tire tread marks, and he'd never have found my dead deer and the rabbit snare unless he fell over them." He stared at his gnarled fingers. "Got a touch of arthritis. Means a storm's coming. Most likely a blizzard. The thing to do first is make that clubhouse weatherproof. And I know how. Jim Frayne knows as much as I did when I was a boy of his age, but don't forget that I've learned a lot since. If I had a horse now, I'd ride over to that clubhouse and teach Jim a few tricks."

"Oh, oh," Honey cried. "I'm so glad you know how to ride, Mr. Maypenny. Daddy'll buy you a horse as soon as you accept the job, but right now you take Strawberry—the roan. Trixie and I'll take turns riding back on Lady. Won't we, Trix?"

Trixie shook her head and carefully strapped Bobby's compass around her wrist. "You ride to the clubhouse with Mr. Maypenny, Honey. I feel like walking—and thinking. It's all so wonderful, I don't want to hurry."

Snow and Surprises • 20

THE BLIZZARD started with a snow flurry around nine o'clock that night. Trixie fell asleep without any worries because, thanks to Mr. Maypenny, the clubhouse was as tight as a drum. The whole day had been so wonderful that she tried to stay awake as long as she could so she could think over all the nice things that had happened.

In the first place, Bobby had been so delighted when she gave him back his compass that he rushed to his mother, confessing and crying in a loud voice: "Oh, I'm such a bad, bad boy! I tookted Trixie's ring and losted it, but she didn't get mad, 'cause it wasn't the right ring. The *right* ring 'longs to Mr.

Lytell on account of Brian's car. But it really 'longs to Trixie, so I'm going to get it back when I give him my squirrel-bird."

He went on with his strange and garbled version, chanting loudly every now and then, "Old lamps for new. Old lamps for *new*. Hey! I'm Aladdin."

So, in the end, Trixie had had to explain the whole transaction to her parents. To her relief, they were very sympathetic and did not scold her at all.

"You're a banker at heart, Trix," Mr. Belden said cheerfully. "But next time you want to borrow money on that ring, I hope you will consult me. Poor Mr. Lytell! He must have been flabbergasted when you made him take it as security."

"I've always said he was a very nice man," Mrs. Belden said, "and I wouldn't be at all surprised if he and Miss Trask got married someday. Also," she finished rather smugly, "I never objected to Ben Riker. He really is a sweet boy. You can't expect an only child to be as well-adjusted as one with—"

"Siblings," Trixie finished, giving her mother a hug. "I'm so glad there are so many siblings in this family and that nobody's mad at me."

Feeling very close to tears of sheer joy, Trixie had rushed up to her room. It was then that she noticed that big, fluffy flakes of snow were falling. The wind came up as rapidly as the temperature dropped, and the snowflakes were turned to swirling, dancing masses of powdered sugar.

When she awoke in the morning, the sun was shining with dazzling brightness on the thick white carpet that covered the ground and almost every inch of the pine and spruce trees. Trixie dressed hurriedly and dashed out to join her brothers.

"Perfect sledding weather," Brian said. "When I get my car, Trix, I'll drive up and down the Wheelers' driveway until the snow is hard-packed." He gave her a hug. "Thanks to you, I can get my jalopy right after breakfast."

"How come?" Trixie asked. "Our week isn't up until this evening. If I remember right, we started last Sunday morning."

"True," Mart put in, "but we can't patrol today. Not on horseback in this deep snow."

"Miss Trask and Mr. Maypenny arranged it all last night after you went home, Trix," Brian told her. "He assured her that we were in for a blizzard, so she gave me a check then and there. All it amounts to is this: We owe Mr. Maypenny a day's work. He says he'd rather have it strung out in hours, here and there. And, best of all, Jim has a permanent job with him as part-time assistant gamekeeper."

"Swell," Trixie cried enthusiastically. "How does Regan like Mr. Maypenny? That's important."

"They're crazy about each other," Mart replied.

"Not that it really matters. They won't see much of each other, because Mr. Maypenny is going to keep his horse in a stall on his own place, which we promised to help him build. We owe him something for the work he did on the clubhouse yesterday. What a man! As nimble as a monkey, and a wizard with carpentry tools."

Trixie nodded. "Is it really all settled then? I mean, what if Mr. Wheeler disapproves of it when he comes back?"

"He called up Honey last night while we were all there," Mart said. "Just to say hello and that he and Mrs. Wheeler would arrive this afternoon unless there was a blizzard. Honey and Miss Trask and Mr. Maypenny all talked to him, so it was settled before he hung up. I gather Mr. Wheeler was so pleased all he could say, to the tune of about forty dollars, was 'Yes, yes, by all means.' Mr. Wheeler is no fool. He knows he's lucky to get a man like Mr. Maypenny."

"He sure is," Trixie agreed. "I can't wait to talk to Honey about it." They hurried in for breakfast then, and afterward Trixie did her chores as fast as she could. Then she pulled on rubber boots and plowed her way up the hill to the Manor House.

Jim and Ben were shoveling paths from the house to the driveway, and the girls were inspecting the snowshoes they had brought up from the clubhouse.

The moment Honey caught sight of Trixie she called out, "Guess what!"

"I don't have to guess," Trixie panted. "The boys just told me *all*. It's too, too good to be true."

"But the boys don't know," Honey replied, sliding along one of the slippery paths to meet Trixie halfway. "Not about Celia and Tom, anyway."

"Oh," Trixie asked, "are they back?"

Honey nodded. "They arrived around midnight, but, even with chains, Tom couldn't get up the driveway, so their car is parked down by the mailbox."

"Oh, dear," Trixie moaned. "If the roads are that bad, then Brian won't be able to drive his car home from Mr. Lytell's, after all."

"Yes, he can," Jim assured her. "The snowplow just went through. It's only our driveway that's hopeless. We've got to fix it so cars can get in and out."

"Let's don't and say we did," Ben said with a grin. "If I can't get out, I'll have to stay here, and that suits me just fine."

"But you've got to be back in school tomorrow evening at the latest," Di pointed out.

"Well, if I can't, I can't," he said cheerfully.

"I know just how you feel," Trixie told him, chuckling. "I wanted the roads to be okay for Brian's sake, but I was hoping maybe we'd get a thaw and then a freeze tomorrow night so the school bus wouldn't run on Monday."

"Instead," Jim said, looking up at the sky, which was now filled with scudding clouds, "I think we're going to get more snow."

"Then there's no sense in shoveling the driveway," Trixie cried enthusiastically. "Let's fix it so it'll be good for sledding. Brian planned to drive his car up and down until the snow was hard-packed, but I guess that's out."

"It's too soft for anything but snowshoes," said Honey, demonstrating. Di *tried* to demonstrate but lost her balance and pitched headfirst into the bank of snow that lay beside the path.

Jim and Ben hastily extricated her, but she was laughing so hard she couldn't stand up. "You can have these snowshoes," she finally told Trixie. "I'm sure I'll never learn how to manage them."

Just then Tom came snowshoeing down from the *Robin*, dragging a big sled behind him. "Hi," he yelled to Trixie. "Did you hear about my deer?"

"No," she yelled back. "Did you get one?"

"That's what I was trying to tell you," Honey said. "The carcass is down in the car, and Tom's afraid somebody will steal it."

Regan, wearing snowshoes, too, appeared then. "Nobody's going to steal that deer," he said emphatically. "And we're going to live on venison stew all winter. Aren't we, Tom?"

"We sure are," Tom replied.

"You'd better get the recipe from Mr. Maypenny," Trixie and Honey said in unison.

"From whom?" Tom asked curiously.

Everybody tried to answer him at once.

"I thought he was a poacher," Trixie said.

"He's our new gamekeeper," Honey said.

"A great guy," Regan said.

"You'll like him a lot," Jim said.

"He wears the oddest clothes," Di said.

"He's terrific!" Ben said.

Tom ignored the jumble of words and said to Regan, "Those kids never did make sense. Let's go get that deer. Maypenny, indeed! Why, nobody around here has a name like that."

Regan guffawed. "It's an old Hudson River valley name, I'll have you know, and he is our new gamekeeper and a great guy, to boot." They went on down the driveway with the sled sliding after them.

Celia poked her head out of the kitchen door then. "Hello, Trix. You and your brothers, Bobby included, are invited for lunch. Miss Trask just talked to your mother, and Mart is on his way up now with Bobby."

"Wonderful," Trixie cried. "Did Moms say anything about Brian and his car?"

"I wouldn't know." Celia shivered and ducked back into the kitchen.

Honey stared at Trixie. "I should think at this

point you'd be more worried about your ring than Brian's car. How and when are you going to get it back?"

"Brian will bring it home with his jalopy, of course," Trixie said. "Dad and Moms know *all*, and they're not mad at me, thank goodness." She turned to Jim. "Brian keeps on thanking me because Mr. Lytell didn't sell the car to a secondhand dealer, but he should really thank you. If it hadn't been for that ring you gave me, Jim—"

"What's all this about a ring?" Ben interrupted. "It sounds as though you were engaged or something."

Trixie sniffed. "If Jim were the last man on earth, I wouldn't marry him."

"Is that so?" Jim gave her a gentle push, and Trixie found herself sitting in the snowbank with Di. She tried to scramble to her feet, but her boots kept slipping on the icy path, so she only went down deeper.

"Do you think I'd get myself engaged to anybody as dumb as that?" Jim asked Ben.

"No," Ben admitted. "But why did you give her a ring? I wouldn't even give her a ring on the phone."

"Oh, stop it," Honey pleaded. "Why must all of you tease Trixie from morning to night? She's the one who always solves all of our problems. And you know it," she finished stormily.

Jim relented then and helped Trixie to her feet. "On you," he said, "snow looks good. You should wear it more frequently. Especially on your eyelashes. Much more becoming than mascara."

Trixie angrily chattered her teeth at him. "Thanks to you, I'm soaked to the skin. If I'd known you were going to be so uncouth, I'd have worn my ski pants instead of jeans. Now I'll have to go home to change. And I'll get that ring, too, Jim Frayne, and give it back to you. I wouldn't be caught dead with it."

"Before you do anything," Ben insisted, "tell me the story of the ring. I'm dying of curiosity."

"If you'll get me out of this snowbank and these snowshoes," Di said, "I'll tell you the story, but only over a cup of hot chocolate."

Trixie started off toward the path that led down to the hollow, but Honey grabbed her arm. "Oh, don't go home," she begged. "I've got a darling snowsuit that will just fit you." She added to Jim, "Let's all go in and have some hot chocolate."

"Suits me." He bent over to untie the thongs on Honey's snowshoes. "Hot chocolate, indeed! I wonder how long it will be before Trixie gets us all in hot *water* again."

Trixie scooped up a handful of the melting snow. "How would you like some icy water down your neck right now?" she asked in a threatening tone of voice. But deep down inside she asked herself a different question: Was another adventure waiting around the corner for them? Trixie sighed happily and sincerely hoped so.